A *Savage* VALENTINE'S DAY

Recipe For A Disaster

A NOVEL BY

KENDRA RAINEY-KING

CHAPTER 1

Blood, Sweat and Tears...

"Hold her legs down bro," Charles yelled to Alex. "Hold her arms," he demanded as he grabbed my arms tightly.

"If this bitch keeps screaming bro, I swear I'm going to kill her!" Dameon shouted as the echo filled the room.

"Shut the fuck up and do what I tell you to do or you're dead!"

I couldn't see anything because I was blindfolded. The only thing I felt was my clothes being tugged on and my legs being torn apart. I prayed to God that this was all just a dream and I would wake up from this tragic reality.

Why was this happening to me? Was it because I didn't clean my room or do my chores? Was it because I forgot to do my bible study homework? Different thoughts crossed my mind as tears escaped my eyes, falling down my cheek. I didn't know why I was being tortured or what I did wrong, but the boys I thought were my true friends turned out to be the worst.

It was only my freshman year in high school and I had no clue on the changes that were about to embark in my life.

"Ahhhhhhhhhhhh!" I screamed as I bit his hand. I felt my legs being pulled apart as someone rammed three fingers inside of me, after pulling my panties to the side. I didn't know who it was; I tried to hear a voice and match it with the volume of his body build.

I knew exactly who they were, but I never thought in a million years that people I trusted would be the same ones to hurt me deeply. I wanted to know what was going on, but I knew that I couldn't, so I tried my best to remember their scents, voices and most of all the pain of what was next to come. I tried to move my head to peek out of the blind fold, but it was on entirely too tight to budge.

"Hold her legs, tighter," Charles demanded.

Charles was the most popular quarterback, a senior on his way to greatness with a full-ride to Wesley to play football. He was stoutly built with a nasty odor that made me want to puke. He ripped my Hanes panties, threw them on the floor, placed on a condom on his small dick, and forced himself inside of me.

My tears were flowing like a river at this point. The pain was indescribable, knowing there was nothing that I could do to make him stop. He kept going until he came, giving me relief as I continued to cry and moan. "You did good," he stated as he patted my shoulder and kissed my forehead. It was a sick way of endearment for him. His breathe smelled just like disgusting beer and salty peanuts.

"You're next, Dameon," he called to him as if he was across the room.

I moved my head quickly, with effort to try to see from under the blindfold but there was no luck. I was still being pent down by two other boys that were stronger than I could ever imagine.

"How did she feel?" he asked, walking closer to me. I could feel him brush up against my skin as he lay on top of me. He rubbed himself across my lips and against my clit.

"She felt good," Charles snickered as he patted Dameon on his back. It only let me know that Alex and Carter were the ones holding me down. "They do say that ugly girls have the best pussy," he mentioned with a grunt as he plunged himself inside of me.

How could they do this to me? I thought as tears ran down my eyes, flowing like a river.

I felt pressure to my neck; Dameon was choking me as he entered me. He placed his hand over my mouth as I cried harder and smelled the disgusting smell on his hands. It was an odor that I'd never smelt before, but he rammed himself inside of me again harder and harder. He was bigger than Charles. I could tell the difference as I tried to fight him.

"Fucking bitch," he moaned as he slapped my face. "You got all this nasty blood on my dick." He slapped one of the guy's hands as I heard the noise. "She was good," he grinned as he pulled out of me and jumped up. He didn't use a condom. I was crying so hard that snot was pouring out of my nose and into my mouth, causing me to choke.

Whamp! I felt a fist to my face as I fainted. I could hear the voices and feel the other two boys continuing to rape me. Alex was speaking in Spanish as he raped me, but I was so out of it at this point. I stopped fighting and let them do whatever they wanted to me because I had no control anyway.

"Damn, why do y'all have to hit her like that?" Carter asked irritated.

"Do what the fuck we tell you to do," Alex demanded.

For a moment, the room became quiet and I couldn't hear anything but my heart beating rapidly. Thump. Thump. Thump. My heart was beating so fast, I thought it was about to explode.

Drip. Drip. Drip. The sounds of the water from the faucet in the vacant house were becoming louder and louder. I was so scared that my legs were trembling and shaking.

I didn't hear any voices for at least thirty minutes and there was no one holding me down on the disgusting air mattress that was on the floor.

"Hello?" I yelled as I kicked and moved my arms, practically fighting the air. I waited for a response, but there was nothing. I didn't feel a breeze from someone walking near me or hear their voices any longer. Nevertheless, I was petrified at this point and trembling as I stood up, preparing myself to remove the blindfold from across my eyes as I urinated a little on myself.

I took a deep breath as I slowly removed the blindfold. I sighed with relief as I walked to the door, opened it slowly, and walked through the kitchen. I didn't know if they were all gone, but I was just glad to be alive. I had no underwear on, nothing but my bra. I didn't think about anything but leaving as blood creeped down my legs mixed with urine. I unlocked the front door...

"Where do you think you are going?" Alex smiled as he walked closer and placed his hand in front of the door. He waved my underwear in my face as he smiled and placed them back in his pocket. He was bigger than me and stronger than me. I was trembling and shaking at this point. There was nothing that I could do to get away from this situation and nothing in sight to pick up and hit him in the head with.

"Please just let me go," I cried. "I want to go home. I won't tell anyone," I pleaded.

"Do you really think that anyone would believe you? We are the stars of the team here and the city praises us for everything we do." He laughed as he grabbed my neck. "I'm not done with you yet; let's have some more fun."

He dragged me to the mattress as he continued to torture me for round two. I guess the other guys had enough because they didn't come back.

He was right though; everything he said was true. The city we lived in cherished these basketball and football stars like they were gods. There was a party for every win, a parade for each victory and a television recognition for each star player. They never had to worry about life or even women for that matter, which boggled me why they did this to me.

I couldn't tell anyone because I was scared at the time, and I knew what type of power they possessed. I knew I would never be the same again after this and it would affect me for the rest of my life.

I cried as I ran home with my torn dress exposing my thighs. As soon as I made it to the house, I thought about climbing into my window, but I didn't see her car parked out front and remembered that she was at bible study. So, I grabbed the extra key from under our rug in the front and twisted the key inside for the door to open. I locked the door in a hurry behind myself and ran to my room as I tore off the rest of the dress that was barely hanging on me.

I ran to the backyard in search of somewhere to store the bloody dress. I couldn't put it in the trash because Mom was too nosey. I couldn't put it in the garage anywhere because she would see it. I glanced at the barbeque pit for a second and remembered how the neighbors were always using her pit without asking. So, I picked up the lighter fluid and noticed it was empty. Next, I placed the bloody dress inside and lit the dress with the lighter as I closed the top. The dress wouldn't burn correctly, and I heard a car approaching, so I grabbed the dress and scurried back inside of the house with the dress in tow. I found a trash bag in the cabinet in the kitchen and placed it in my room, under my bed.

I couldn't stop thinking and wanting to know why this was happening to me. I was the only child and my mother's pride and joy. I couldn't do anything but think as I took a hot shower and cried, remembering what was done to me and watching it replay repeatedly in my head. I scrubbed myself so hard that I began to hurt, so I turned the water off and decided to run a hot bath to soak instead.

As I sat in the scorching water, the red and purple marks against my skin caused to me sink into the water. I tried to drown myself. I wanted to be dead and gone so I could never see those boys again in my life. For some reason, I couldn't stay under water for long and took a deep gasp for breath as I grabbed a towel.

I noticed next to the towel was the balloon and card from Amauri that said, *Happy Valentine's Day—you're something special.* I cried as I threw the card down and looked at myself in the mirror.

I looked at my dark skin, big, stretched nose and big lips. *Why me God?* I asked out loud as I turned around and looked inside every cabinet in my bathroom. *I don't deserve to live. I am ugly, I am ruined, and now I am dead inside,* I thought to myself as I looked for something to drown my sorrow with.

I walked into the kitchen, opened a bottle of my mother's hidden Hennessy, and poured me a cup. As I opened the liquor cabinet, I noticed a small grey razor. I grabbed it and placed the Hennessy back into the cabinet as I walked back to my room and made my way inside of the bathroom.

After drinking the Hennessy halfway, I positioned a small bath towel into my mouth and bit into it as I slowly cut across both of my wrists. Both of my arms were dangling from the bathtub as I stared into the ceiling; blood dripped slowly from my wrists as I began to fade away.

CHAPTER 2

Everybody Ain't Your Friend...

Four months ago...before life changed for good...

"Girl, put those dolls away! You're in the ninth grade now and it's time for you to throw them away," Mama stated as she walked into my room, only to see me playing dress up with my dolls.

"I was just changing their clothes," I tried to explain.

"I know, and I also know that that your imagination is high," Mama explained. "I heard you this morning, projecting different voices and disguising yourself...I just really think it's time to put those dolls away and get you some real friends."

"I don't know Mama," I said calmly. "People don't like me too much and think that I am weird. I had no friends in middle school and I am scared to make friends."

"Baby, I just want you to at least try. I know it's been hard since your dad passed when you were in the fifth grade and life changed so much. But, I am so proud of you and how God has stepped into your life. You have been so adamant about going to bible study and learning more about the Lord, but I want you to also enjoy your adolescence."

"Okay Mama, for you I will try to make friends."

"Good, and they are putting you in some advanced classes as well so don't be afraid of the upperclassmen and don't let them push you around."

"I won't," I promised.

"Don't be mad at what I'm about to do because it needs to be done," Mom explained as she grabbed all thirteen of my dolls and threw them away in the trashcan outside.

I didn't put up a fight because I guess Mama was right. It was time for me to be a big girl and I was surprised that she was the one pushing me to be one. All I ever knew was church. We went to church seven days a week because Mama was on the board. She was an Apostle with different views on life that sometimes I didn't understand, but I was brought up to honor and respect it.

I stood up and stared at myself in the mirror. I hated myself. I hated the skin that I was in. I was picked on all my life from kids at every school I attended. I couldn't catch a break wherever I went. I didn't like how I appeared and I couldn't stand having curves and a big ass.

I was told that I was ugly, had bad skin, couldn't be seen at night and that I would never be liked. Therefore, I never had friends wherever I went and moved to different schools just because of the bullying.

We lived in Dallas, Texas in one of the biggest houses in the Turtle Creek area. Most started off in the $609.9K price range with the luxury of five to seven bedrooms. Mom wanted a five-bedroom, four bath with a four-car garage.

She got exactly what she wanted and moved us from the ghetto slums of Dallas to the elite suburbs when I was ten, and we've been here ever since. My father was a hard-worker with his own engineering and construction company that built the biggest buildings in Texas.

He fell off a building Downtown, crushed his head in, and broke almost every bone in his body. The city takes care of us until the day we die after that, and when Mom received the first settlement check from the city, she moved us without any hesitation.

We were definitely living in luxury but, unfortunately, I was unhappy with myself and it was going to take a lot more than a mansion sized home to make me feel alive.

First day of school....

"Why the hell did they put a freshman in our Media Business class?" Dameon asked out loud, while our teacher was still waiting for the rest of the students to come inside after the first bell. He was shaking his head with pure disgust as he stared at me.

"I don't know, but she ugly as fuck," Charles replied.

"She ain't real ugly; she just dresses like a grandma," Alex laughed as he tapped Charles on the shoulder.

I heard them laughing and giggling as they talked about me,

amongst themselves. I wasn't brave enough to confront them and I hated this about myself. Mrs. Arnold walked into the classroom and instruction began.

The guys began to throw spitballs into my hair. I turned around to acknowledge them and they all began to laugh as if it was funny. Mrs. Arnold, a preppy and young Caucasian woman shook her head with disgust.

"You might as well just suck it up and finish your work," the girl next to me stated as she tried to whisper to me.

"Huh?" I asked with disbelief.

"I know that you don't know me, but you are the new girl and you're a freshman in this class."

"What does that mean?" I asked impatiently.

"Let me see your schedule," she asked as she took it from my desk and looked at it. "Oh, you have B lunch; sit by me, and by the way, I'm Karen."

"I'm Charisma." I replied, nice to meet you.

Karen wasn't a looker herself. She was a big girl with big moles on her face and smeared red-lipstick across her teeth in the front. She was black and white but wasn't blessed in the looks department at all. We were both a mess together I assumed. I laughed at her corny jokes as she passed me a piece of gum.

I smiled as I placed my schedule back onto my desk. The boys were still throwing spitballs into my hair, but I decided the best solution was to just ignore them.

Lunch...

"How were your other classes?" Karen asked me as I sat down next to her at the lunch table.

"They were okay, but the school is so big that I was lost and was late to every class," I explained.

"It's your first day and you're a freshman."

"What does that mean?" I asked.

"Basically, it's just your insurance to be able to be late all week," she laughed.

"Oh, okay," I giggled. "So, what grade are you in?"

"I'm in the eleventh, so one more year in this stupid ass school and I am out of here," she boasted.

"Lucky you," I chimed in.

"I'm going to college far away where I never have to worry about those stupid ass football players who get to do whatever the hell they want."

"Why is that?" I questioned as I took a bite of the spaghetti and corn on my tray.

"Rich ass parents," she replied. "Their parents have money invested into the school and I'm not talking about thousands."

"Wow!"

"Yea, and those same guys throwing spit balls, they are the worst guys you will ever meet. Not to mention, they have had mostly every girl in the school. Everything is given to them on a platter and they don't take no for an answer."

"Well, my mother is wealthy too," I tried to explain until the infamous crew walked to different tables, taking rolls and juices off different student's lunch trays.

I cringed as they walked to our table and held my head down as one of them stood directly in the front of me.

"I need you to do my math work for me," he demanded as he threw it near my tray. "It better be done by first period."

He walked away as the other boys followed. I looked on his math paper and saw the name *Amauri* written at the top. I repeated his name out loud but not enough for them to hear me.

"He's not like the others. I don't even know why he wants to fit in with those stupid, cock suckers."

"Whoa, language," I insinuated.

"Oh please, don't tell me that you are one of those no cursing, believe in Jesus people?"

"I don't ever leave home without my bible."

"We will see how long that lasts here."

I had no clue of what she meant, but she warned me of different things on my first day to take heed to. I wondered in my head could there be a way to turn Amauri around. I wondered if I could introduce him to the Lord and quite possibly be his friend as well.

CHAPTER 3

The Secret

Things didn't quite pan out as I wanted them to. Amauri wasn't receptive to my conversations about the Lord. But, we were in two classes together. Karen and I both had to do their work for them even though we only shared the media and gym class together. Amauri and I never talked in the media class, but he always seemed to talk to me in gym.

Gym was the only class that I dreaded. I was failing because I never dressed up and I never tried to do anything in the class. It was so many students in the class that it made my head spin. I tried my best to hide close to the bleachers, so I wouldn't be picked during volleyball and basketball games. I was so nervous about everything and my mind would take me to the darkest places.

"Student fails to dress out and participate!" Mom yelled as I walked through the door. She was holding the progress report with sadness as she looked at me. "What's going on with you?"

"I..."

"Do you not like the school or something?" she asked as she took a seat on the couch. "I just can't do this anymore; it's very tiresome moving you from school to school. You're going to have to stick up for yourself,"

"Yes, ma'am," I replied as I walked to my room. I knew deep down that she was right, but it was apparent that the school was ran by these boys and there was nothing she could do. I didn't want to disappoint her because she seemed to be tired and weary lately. I didn't know what was going on, but she didn't seem herself and even slowed down from attending church on a regular basis.

A week later...

I was so excited because I was finally going to get these braces off that I'd had since fifth grade. I was so ecstatic as I came dashing out of my room.

"Are you ready?" Mom asked as she sat on the couch.

"Yes, I am so ready, Mommy!"

"Oh, shoot!" she yelled as we walked to the door in unison and she reached inside of her purse.

"What's wrong?" I asked.

"I left my dog-on wallet on my dresser upstairs," she grunted as she headed into the directions of the stairs.

"Don't worry about it Mama, I'll get it," I assured her as I ran past her and up the stairs.

I hit the light switch in search for her wallet on her dresser and there was a paper right next to the wallet. As soon as I saw who it was from, I opened it. Tears ran down my cheek creating a puddle on her dresser. I couldn't believe what was happening; my mother had a letter from the Cancer Center of Dallas telling her that she was in her last stages of cancer. She had no more than six months to live. Life as I knew it was about to change even worse than I could ever imagine.

CHAPTER 4

School Daze...

I didn't tell my mother that I knew about her big secret. I was scared to say anything, and the dentist informed me that I still would need another twelve months for my braces. My day was completely messed up at that point. I sat on the bleachers during fifth period in gym and watched the girls and boys play volleyball together with their shorts on.

"Charisma, you're going to have to dress out today," Coach Emily stated as she walked up to me and closed my folder.

"I can't do that," I tried to explain. "Those shorts are something I refuse to wear."

"Well, you can take that up with the Principal because I won't have anyone in this gym who refuses to participate. You need a year of gym and if you make another zero, your first six weeks won't look good at all and the school will kick you out."

"I can't allow that to happen," I cried.

"Well, go dress out Charisma; the clothes are in your locker," she suggested. "No one will be staring at you when all of you are wearing the same things."

I placed my folder in my backpack as I made my way to the locker room. I didn't want to show my body in those shorts and have everyone look at me. I was so nervous and beyond petrified as I opened my locker and began to change clothes. I didn't want to disappoint my mother again and make her transfer me when she had cancer. I knew my mother was already stressed and sick; this wouldn't make her any better.

I opened the door nervously to go back into the gym and everyone was still playing volleyball on one side and basketball on the other. Amauri was the first one to catch a glimpse; as I walked by him, he was staring so hard that the basketball hit him in the face. Everyone was laughing as he tried to play it off. His entire crew was watching: Carter, Alex, Charles, and Dameon.

As I walked to the bench, all eyes were on me and I didn't like it all. I wasn't the one to be the light on a stage. I was more of the voice behind the curtains.

"Damn girl, I didn't know you were shaped like that," Karen goofed as she sat next to me. "Everybody talking about your body."

I put on my jacket as she continued to talk. "Don't cover yourself; what are you ashamed for?"

"I just don't like people looking at me," I explained. "I'm ugly and now since I started my period in the sixth grade, I have these huge, ugly ass bumps on my face and my hips and butt have spread like my mother's."

"And you're complaining because?"

"I just feel ashamed."

"Ashamed? For what? You have one of the best bodies at school and here I am looking like a fat and black Rosie O' Donnell. The acne will eventually go away."

We both laughed as the coach walked near us. "Okay girls, both of you are in the next game. Get ready!"

I nodded my head as I stood up and took my jacket off. I didn't like the attention but maybe Karen was right. I needed to loosen up some and get myself together. I was sheltered a lot at home and homeschooled until fourth grade, so everything was a big deal to me and I had a hard transition.

Amauri sat down as I played with the rest of the boys and watched me play. I did great for my first time playing. I just wished that everyone would stop staring at me. It was a generational curse that I couldn't stand, and it was the same reason why I wore big dresses and pantsuits to school.

After the game was over, I rushed past everyone to change clothes before anyone would come in. I opened the locker to retrieve my clothes and stared at myself in the mirror. I had the perfect body: thighs, butt, hips, and even my breasts filled out nicely. My only thought now was looking at my dark skin, bumpy face, and long ass nose. Ugh. I closed the locker swiftly as I changed clothes and grabbed my backpack as the other girls entered.

"I was wondering where you went," Karen stated as she opened her locker and began to converse with me. She just started taking off her clothes and she got naked.

"Are you not ashamed?" I asked in disbelief.

"Why should I be?" she asked with a smirk. "I have the same as any other girl in here but just a little bit more."

"The girls, they will talk about you," I whispered.

"I don't care," she stated nonchalantly. "I have worse things to worry about right now."

"But you don't care about what they say?"

"Absolutely not, if I cared, I would be a mental patient by now," she explained as she pulled up her pants and we darted to the door to make it on time to our next class before the bell rung.

Karen had so much confidence and she didn't care who looked at her. I wanted to be like that, but I was too ashamed. Maybe one day, I would gather up enough courage to be free from the thoughts and likings of others. Hell, I was only a freshman.

The next day...

"Come sit down and talk to me," Mom suggested as I opened the door and saw her sitting on the couch. She had a piece of paper in her hand and I nervously sat down on the floor next to her.

"What's wrong Mama?" I asked, softly.

"I didn't want to scare you and thought that I would be okay and handle it by praying."

"What's going on?" I asked as I stared into her eyes.

"I'm dying, baby."

"Mama, please don't say that."

"It's true," she stated as tears streamed down her eyes. "I found out the reason I have been feeling so sick and sluggish. I have known for a few months now, but God is still allowing me to live."

"It's cancer, Mama?"

"Yes, it is."

I promised my mother that I would be there for her in every step of the way. I was so scared for my mother because she wasn't the same person anymore and began to get real sick. I don't understand why she didn't want to take chemo to help, but she decided against it.

The doctor gave her different pills to make her comfortable. Life before I knew it was already changing drastically. We weren't close with my father's side of the family and my mother's side barely came around unless they wanted something. The only person that could look after me was my aunt Jasmine and she was doing her last year of college at Spelman. I didn't think she would come back to Texas and take care of me if anything ever happened to my mother, but Mom assured me that she would. After this series of events, I began to keep a journal every day to write down my feelings and thoughts.

This was definitely a low place for me because I was confused on not only my life but worried about my mother's.

A month later...

"Can I see your notes?" Amauri asked as he sat next to me in class. I was surprised that he sat next to me.

"Sure," I replied as I handed it to him and he thanked me as he moved back to his assigned seat.

Karen was sick lately and was barely at school. I called her for the last two days and she didn't answer. I stared at her empty seat and prayed that she was okay.

Amauri became the guy that slipped letters into my locker, carried my books to my classes, and offered me his seat at lunch. I would sneak just to call him late at night just to tell him good night. Whenever I talked to him, my heart simply skipped a beat. I would think about him day in and day out. Two weeks had passed and Amauri asked me to meet him after class by my locker.

The bell rung for next period and I jumped up to scurry to my locker. I placed my journal in my locker and closed it. Dameon was standing right on the other side of the locker. I took a deep breath as he stared at me.

"What's up?" he asked.

"Nnnn...Nothing," I stuttered.

"I want to take you to the *Sadie Hawkins* dance that's coming up," he stated with clarity, as if I didn't have a choice in the matter.

"Me?" I questioned.

"Do you see me talking to anyone else?" he asked rudely as he walked closer to me.

I didn't like the look in his eyes. It was something about his black and deceitful eyes that I didn't like. My mother told me boys with the name Dameon, Damion and Damon were the sons of the devil and to watch out for them.

"No, thanks," I stated as I walked off.

"What? You are dissing me?" he asked loudly.

I kept walking as he came behind me. "Did you hear what I said?" he asked as he turned me around to face him.

"Dude, what are you doing?" Amauri asked as he came into my defense. "Let her be."

A week later, the boys who gave me the hardest times were all being nice to me. Except for Dameon; he stayed back in his seat during class and didn't utter a single word to me, and I was fine with that. I opened up a little more and began to actually show them how to do their work, as opposed to me doing it for them.

"Mom, I really like school now!" I said, excited as I kissed her cheek while she lay on the couch.

"That's so good baby," she replied, coughing roughly.

"Are you okay, Mama?"

"I am baby," she smiled. "I stay prayed up and I got the Lord on my side."

"Yes, ma'am." I kissed her cheek again. "I'll get dinner started."

"When did you become this young woman, taking care of your mama like this?" she asked proudly as she sat up and flipped the channel.

"New beginnings I guess, Mama."

"I take it school is going well now and those crazy kids aren't bullying you anymore," she quizzed.

"No more bullying, Mama," I acknowledged as I walked into the kitchen and began to prepare spaghetti and meatballs for dinner. "Mama, can we go shopping for more clothes?"

She stood up from the couch in shock. "Huh? You want to go shopping?" she asked with a surprised tone.

"Yes, ma'am," I replied as she walked into the kitchen to join me. "I want to look different Mama. I want to change up my look a little."

"It must be a boy," she smiled.

"Kind of."

"Well, I guess it's time we had the big talk."

"Oh, Lord," I huffed as I sat down in the chair.

"Don't do that; it's about time and you're in the ninth grade now. Boys only want one thing Charisma and I want you to grow up and be strong like me. I only had one sexual experience with a man and that man was your father. He wined and dined me like a true gentleman and I was in love. It was how I knew that when he got on his knees and asked me to marry him that it was the right thing to do. I was the only girl who wasn't running around and being fast at your age. My oldest sister, she was pregnant at 13 and left to fend on her own. These boys in this generation are not only cruel, but they don't have respect for women anymore. I can't tell you how many young girls used to come to the church and pray against those sins and fornications. You are blessed to have a body like your mother, but you have to be careful in how you use it."

"Mama what do you mean?"

"You have the body of a grown woman and you will tempt many boys and even men," she replied. "It is why I keep you covered and why you are covered in the blood."

"Mama, I just wanted new clothes; it doesn't have to show my figure."

"Okay baby, but I don't want you dressed up like those jezebels."

"I promise I won't."

"I'm not feeling good, so we will have to go this weekend."

"I really need a new wardrobe," I replied sadly. "Can I please go by myself?"

It took her a moment to respond and I didn't think she was quite ready to trust me. Hell, I didn't trust myself, but I wanted freedom and the ability to do something for myself. She gave me seven hundred dollars to go shopping with and I was ecstatic. I caught the bus to North Park Mall after I was done cooking dinner.

I tried on different dresses at the stores and found so many outfits to compliment my figure. I tried to buy some of the dresses she would like because I knew that I could put the dress on before I left for school and change as soon as I got there.

I walked inside of different stores, carrying all of my bags and bought myself a slice of pepperoni pizza. A guy was standing next to the pizza stand with different bottles of Proactive. I had seen all of the commercials, so I bought a few to try and prayed for a miracle as I exited the mall because it was 8:00 p.m. and only two more buses ran for the remainder of the night.

I took the last bite of my pizza as I looked across the street and saw Karen coming out of the *Family Care Pregnancy Center* building. She walked across the street and ran to the bus stop.

"Hey, Karen," I said as she looked up at me.

"Oh, hey," she replied. The look upon her face didn't read happy as she turned around swiftly, trying to hide her bag.

The bus came quickly, and she jumped on the bus as I searched for my day pass inside of my purse. I sat next to her and I could sense that she was rolling her eyes as she sucked her teeth.

"I've been calling you," I whispered.

"New number," she stated.

"Why haven't you been at school?"

"Oh, I don't attend Mercy any longer."

"Oh, okay. So, can I have your new number?"

"Look, you and I are not friends, okay?" she said in a sassy tone. "Plenty of seats on this bus, so find you one."

I jumped up and moved with a vengeance as I sat all the way at the back. I didn't understand why she was so damn mean to me. I didn't say anything else to her as I pressed the button for the next stop in front of my house.

As soon as I made it in the house, I put all my bags down and opened my laptop. I didn't know much about clinics, sex and all of that, but something was telling me that something wasn't right. I searched for the clinic on Google and it was a clinic for pregnant teens only. They only did two things: provided pre-natal care with referrals or abortions.

My eyes grew bigger as I looked at the website. *Karen was pregnant, but why in the blue hell was she upset with me?* I thought as I closed the laptop.

The next day at school, I wore one of my new dresses that hugged the curves of my body. Amauri was being extra friendly, and I laughed as he sat next to me and talked to me. He began to sit in Karen's seat as we worked on a presentation together.

I spent most of my evenings watching the boys practice. We were going to the championship and screamed and hollered in the bleachers as the cheerleaders practiced. Amauri smiled as he stood and stared at me. I was cheering him on as he ran through the field.

"Pathetic," Carmen scolded loudly with her crew as she walked past me. She had the most beautiful green eyes and straight hair. Carmen was Cuban and black with a flat ass, but she was a part of the popular crew. "So, who are you cheering for?"

"Amauri," I replied boastfully.

"In your dreams," she giggled as she mugged me up and down. "Damn, you're dark as night."

I grabbed my backpack and moved to the other side as she continued to talk noise and laugh at me. *Always ignore stupid girls and people who say stupid things.* I remembered the words my mother would tell me, and it seemed to always prepare me for moments like these that would occur in my life.

"What is the definition of stupid ladies?" Carmen shouted to her crew as I looked up. "Give me C-H-A-R-I-S-M-A!" she shouted unto the top of her lungs as she clapped her hands together as if she was a cheerleader.

"Hahaha," I boasted as I stood up and finally decided to leave. I walked down the bleachers as they continued to make fun of me. The game was over anyway and I needed to leave. As I looked down at my watch, it was an hour before my curfew.

"Where are you headed?" Amauri asked as he walked behind me, lifting his helmet off his head.

I couldn't help but to stop and stare at his incredible smile as he spoke to me. His straight, white teeth had me completely mesmerized.

"Thanks for your support today."

"You're welcome."

He followed behind me as I continued to walk under the bleachers. Before I could turn around, he grabbed me from behind and kissed my lips softly. I pushed him back quickly without thinking and looked around to make sure no one was watching. I was trembling and shaking like a leaf on a tree.

"What's wrong?"

"I shouldn't be doing this."

"Are you not attracted to me?"

"Of course, you just took me by surprise,"

"Wait for me here okay," he pleaded. "I'll be right back."

I nodded my head and stared at my watch. I couldn't believe that I had my first kiss. I smiled at the thought as I watched Carmen and her crew from under the bleachers. They didn't see me, but I could see them.

"He would never ever in a million years date her," she implied. "First of all, she is ugly and black as hell. Secondly, she is a freshman and we are all juniors and seniors."

I took off like a rocket with tears rolling down my face and ran until I made it home. I could have been a track star for all I knew because I was gone like hell. I don't know what the kiss was about, but I let Carmen and her nasty friends talking about me, get to me.

***

I avoided Amauri in the hallway the next morning and tried my hardest to move through the crowd swiftly. I didn't want to tell him what I heard, and I definitely was embarrassed for leaving without saying anything.

I sat down in our media class and Amauri was already in the seat next to mine. "I thought something happened to you and I had to call the police to file a missing person's report or something."

I blushed as he moved a hair strand from my face. "I just had curfew," I explained as everyone began to take their seats in the class.

"I really like you," Amauri whispered.

My heart was beating so fast that I could barely think straight. I just kept smiling as he continued to talk but I drifted off into my own thoughts until the damn bell rung for the next period.

"Let me walk you to your class," he insinuated as he grabbed my books.

We turned the corner as I walked to my locker to grab my other spiral notebook. I opened my locker and different types of candy fell to the floor with a balloon and card stuffed inside. Everyone stopped in their tracks to stare at us as the cheerleading team held a big sign that asked: WILL YOU GO TO SADIE HAWKINS WITH ME?

I covered my face and tried to stop the tears from falling down my face. I dropped my purse and ran to the restroom. Amauri looked at me like I was crazy, and I had no clue what to say. I was so embarrassed. I never liked people looking at me for nothing in the world. It truly bothered me. I also knew that I was unable to attend the dance with a boy who was a junior. My mother would flip out completely. I couldn't have a boyfriend or even dress the way that I was at school. Amauri knew certain things that I couldn't do because I would sneak and call him on the home phone almost every night.

Amauri knocked on the restroom door and walked inside. He was just like the other guys at times; it was exactly what Karen meant when she said they did whatever they wanted. It didn't matter what school I went to, boys were not allowed in the girl's restrooms and those were the rules. It was no way around it.

I stood up in the restroom stall and locked the lock. I could see him walk in through the side-holes through the door.

"Out," he pointed to the two girls that were standing in the mirror. "Come out, Charisma," he demanded.

I waited a few seconds to answer until he knocked, and I opened the door. I walked out and stared at him without belting out a word.

"What's wrong with you?" he asked.

"I..I..I..just can't go with you to the dance."

"Why is that?"

"My mama doesn't believe in me dating and she would have a fit if she found out that you are a junior."

"Why does she have to know?"

"What do you mean?"

"Let me do the thinking for you, okay?"

"Amauri, I don't understand."

"Shhh…" he stated as he placed one finger over my mouth to shush me. He pulled me closer into him and kissed my lips softly as my heart began to race. "Just meet me at the dance and we will be together then and our relationship will be a secret from her."

"Really?" I asked with sincerity. "Why me?"

"This…" he stated as he placed his hand over my heart. He kissed me again passionately and this time I kissed him back until two other girls walked in. I looked up and it was Carmen with her mouth open. We walked out as we heard her throw a tantrum in the restroom.

"She really likes you," I said with my head down.

"She's an ex," he explained.

"I heard, and she's beautiful."

"So are you," he replied as he pulled my chin up to look at him.

"You are just saying that to be nice."

"No, I was jerk when we first met but there is something special about you," he smiled. "Carmen thinks the world owes her something because she looks a certain way. In her world, sadly, she believes because we are both popular and fit the description of looks that we belong together."

"You don't want to be with her?"

"Hell no, she is crazy and she thinks just because her brother is my best friend that she will get a pass."

"Her brother?"

"You didn't know?"

"No," I shrugged my shoulder awaiting an answer.

"Her brother is Dameon; we've been friends since elementary."

"Oh wow, I didn't know that."

"Enough about them. I can't wait until the dance; it's going to be special for us."

"I'm so excited…now I have to find something to wear."

"Why don't you wear red?" he suggested.

"Red?" I quizzed.

"It's my favorite color."

"Okay, I'll find something," I assured him.

I couldn't believe that this was happening to me. I was nothing but smiles the entire ride home as my mother picked me up.

"You are in a good mood," Mom recognized.

"I love this school Mama," I smiled.

I just kept thinking about the dance and couldn't wait. I saved

$150 from the money Mom gave me and would ask her for more for shoes. I snuck on the cordless home phone and dialed Amauri's number. We began to talk about the dance, and I was so excited about it.

I had been watching different videos and listening to different songs so I could learn how to slow dance. I secretly twerked with the music low when Mom was sleep or drained from her meds. I was really feeling as if I was about to come out of my shell.

"You there?" Amauri asked. I could feel him smiling as he talked on the phone.

"I'm here," I replied, still in deep thought.

"Oh snap, my boys are calling," Amauri stated as I heard the line click.

"Okay, I'll see you tomorrow. I won't be able to talk later."

"Just hold on a second. I want to talk to them anyway with you on the phone."

I held my breath as I wondered why he needed to have me on the phone with his friends. Sure 'nuff, he came on the line with all four of the boys. They were all being goofy and talking about girls and where they would be going to college at.

"I wanted to let y'all know that I am with Charisma," he blurted out as everyone became quiet.

"So, you with her like for real?" Dameon asked in shock.

"Yep," he replied without hesitation.

Dameon remained quiet on the phone as everyone began to

talk. The other guys replied, "That's what's up," and they moved on to another conversation about football. I guess it was how boys made light of everything. They talked about stuff and moved on from it quickly. Dameon even chimed in now as they continued to converse. I smiled proudly from ear to ear as I plopped on my soft bed.

"What are you wearing to the dance?" Dameon asked Amauri.

"Red and white," he boasted. "You know I have to be on point."

"Yea, yea, yea nigga," he replied sarcastically.

They talked for hours and I either laughed at the jokes or shook my head at what boys talked about over the phone. I ended up falling asleep with my ear to the phone as my mother woke me up the next morning.

"Who were you on the phone with?" Mom asked as she shook me to wake me up.

"No one," I lied as I wiped the slob from my face.

"I hope you're not being fast child. These boys are not worth anything," she stated as she sat down on the bed next to me.

I looked at her pale, dry skin and tried not to cry. My mother was looking so bad and here I was hiding the fact that I had a boyfriend and that I was going to a dance with him. I knew she would half kill me.

"Can we spend time together Mama?" I asked.

"That's a good idea. What do you have in mind?"

"I wanted to get my hair done for the dance Mama and I want to look different."

"Okay, we can do that baby," she smiled. "How do you want it?"

"I saw a style on the internet that liked. It was straight with bangs."

"So, you want to let go of the natural style?"

"Please Mama, I can't do anything with it," I pleaded.

"Okay, let me think about this. You go ahead and get ready for school so I can take you."

"Yes, ma'am," I smiled. I knew that it meant I was going to get my hair bone straight with bangs. I couldn't wait to get a new look, and maybe later on she would allow me to add blonde streaks into it.

***

I walked into my media class and Amauri came trailing behind me. He grabbed my books and backpack as usual as his friends looked at us.

"Look the love birds," Alex goofed as they huddled around us.

"Are you coming to practice today?" Charles asked Amauri.

"Yea for a little while," he answered. "Can you come and support me?" he asked me as he placed his hand on top of mine.

"Of course," I replied.

I watched Amauri as he bounced the ball up and down the court like a mad man. He was dribbling like an NBA player and I was so impressed. I couldn't believe how great he was in not only football but basketball as well.

Dameon had hurt his ankle and seemed upset as he sat next to me. I could feel him looking at me as I stood up to cheer from the bleachers. I looked out of the corner of my eye and could see him practically staring at my butt.

"So, you like Amauri a lot?" he asked as he applied pressure to his ankle with a towel.

"I guess so," I replied as I sat back down on the bleachers.

"Me and you should hang out," he insinuated as he placed his hand on my thigh.

Removing his hand from my thigh anxiously, I replied, "No thanks." He looked at me with the most hateful stare that I had ever seen in my life.

I walked away and moved towards the stand as I purchased a drink and sat somewhere else. I could see Charles now sitting next to Dameon as they both stared at me. It was an awkward stare and quite frankly, one that I would never forget.

An hour later...

Everyone left the stands as I sat in silence waiting for Amauri. I was so excited to hug him after his big win. I was glad that my mother allowed me to stay at school late because she had something to do.

"Thanks for waiting for me," Amauri stated as he gave me a big hug and squeezed me tight. He kissed my cheek so delicately that all I could do was blush. "I got you something."

"Really?" I asked in shock as he grabbed a white box from his backpack.

I took the red ribbon that was tied into a bow off the long, white box. My eyes grew big as I opened it and pulled out the necklace. It was a 24k necklace and the price tag read *$1,230.* I couldn't believe that he spent this amount of money on me. I could barely have $50 in my wallet when I came to school without my mother pitching a fit on learning to budget and stretching out money.

"It's beautiful," I stated as I stared into his glossy eyes.

"Not as beautiful as you," he replied. "Let me," he mentioned as he grabbed the necklace with a heart shape in the middle and diamonds filtered around the core and put it on my neck as I held my hair up for him. "You're special to me."

"Do you know what you want to do when you grow up?" he asked suddenly.

"I want to be one of the biggest fashion designers in the world," I mentioned with a smile as we continued to walk.

Amauri definitely gave me butterflies and I was so excited about the dance. He dropped me off a street over from my house and kissed my lips gently after he opened the car door for me. I opened the door with my keys and was shocked to see my aunt Jasmine sitting on the couch, holding my mother's hand.

"What's going on?" I asked sadly as I dropped my backpack at the door and walked over.

"We need to talk to you," Aunt Jasmine alerted me.

"Okay." I sat on the floor in front of them, Indian-style, as they both stared at me.

"Your mom received some bad news Charisma."

"What kind of bad news?" I asked as tears began to flow down my face like a river.

"The doctor gave me two to three weeks at the most to live baby," Mom stated as tears began to run down her face and she sniffled as she grabbed the Kleenex on the table.

"Mama, I don't want you to die. I can't live without you."

"Baby, this is so hard for me and this cancer is destroying me and taking me down. I am getting weary now and I tried to fight it as long as I could."

"What's going to happen to me Mama? I don't understand; I thought you said that God was your vessel and he would take care and supply all of our needs?" I asked as I continued to cry.

"He is baby and always will be," she cried. "I can't predict the future but your auntie came home just to take care of you."

"Will I have to move to Georgia?"

"There is a great possibility that you will have to."

"I'm almost done with school and your mom had almost paid this beautiful home off, so it will be in your name and it will be yours when you are an adult. I will make the payments with the money from your dad and take over the house until you are able to," Aunt Jasmine assured me as she held my hand.

"So, when Mama goes to heaven, I will be moving to Georgia with you until I am grown?" I asked with shock as I looked at both of them in their eyes.

"Unfortunately, I can't stay in Texas, but I promise as soon as school is finished that I will come back here and you will be back at home."

I felt like my life was over. After they were done talking to me, I walked to my room and cried myself to sleep thinking about my mother and the move. I didn't want to move to Georgia and I hated the fact that other people in the family were so shady because my mother had money. They thought my mother owed them all money and after she didn't pass out money to the family, they just started to act funny with us. I didn't get to see my other aunts, uncles, cousins or anything of that sort. I didn't grow up getting to go over Cousin Stacy's house to spend the weekend and play dolls. I was never able to experience that because of the family beef. It really was no one in the world that I could talk to except my mother, aunt Jasmine and now Amauri.

I woke up to use the bathroom and checked the time on the clock; it read *11:03 p.m.* I opened the door to see both Aunt Jasmine and my mother asleep on the couch. I covered them both with a cover and kissed both of their foreheads as I tip-toed to my room to dial Amauri's number.

"Hey," he answered softly as he turned the volume down on his game. I knew he was up playing, *Grand Theft Auto: 5.* I was usually on the phone with him and his boys as they played the game online and dominated each other as I laughed at their comments.

"I wanted to talk to you about something," I tried to explain.

"OH, SHIT!" he yelled.

"What's wrong?" I asked.

"Nothing baby, I failed the mission," he goofed as he continued to play the game.

"Oh, okay."

"What were you saying?" he asked.

"I will just tell you tomorrow," I tried to explain.

"It must be important. Let me click over and tell the fellas that I will call them back."

"Okay," I smiled.

I waited for him to come back on the line. "Okay, I'm back."

"I just needed to tell you something and it's not good at all."

"What's wrong?"

"My mama is sick and dying from cancer," I cried and sniffled, trying to hold my composure as I sat on the end of the bed.

"Man, I'm so sorry baby. I wish I could see you right now," he replied. "I am going to be here for you every step of the way," he assured me.

"I don't think that can happen," I sniffled.

"Why not? I am a man of my word and my dad taught me to always be that, no matter what, and I will be here for you."

I couldn't do anything but smile but that instantly turned into a frown as I grabbed ahold of the heart pendant dangling from the necklace he gave me and began to speak.

"I am moving to Georgia."

"What?"

"My aunt is here from Georgia and whenever my mom leaves the world then I will be moving with her until she finishes college."

"Wow," he said in a disappointed tone.

"I know and everything is so messed up," I whimpered.

"Dear God, please allow this brave soul and her mother to emerge through this life. Please let her mother get well and break free of cancer within the next visit to the hospital, Amen," he prayed surprisingly out loud as I closed my eyes and recited the same words after him.

"Wow, thank you so much. You sound like a Pastor or something."

He laughed as I continued to talk. "My father is actually a Pastor at Mt. Zion Baptist Church in Desoto so I'm a PK," he assured me.

"What's that?"

"It's just an abbreviation for Preacher's Kid."

"Oh, okay."

"My homies don't understand the church life like that so I make sure that I don't show them that side of me."

"Wow, if they are your real friends, why would you have to hide your true self?" I asked in a surprise tone.

"I can't explain that right now, but there is something that I want you to know."

"What's that?"

"Everything will work out Charisma and we will see each other and be with each other. I have hope and I prayed for a good girl with a good heart who doesn't care about materialistic things and wanted nothing but a good, honest life."

Tears formed in my eyes yet again, as he continued to talk. He had so much wisdom and here I was thinking it would be the other way around. I thought he would be upset with me and most of all, I had all types of thoughts that he would break up with me.

***

I woke up the next day to the aroma of pancakes, bacon, eggs and grits throughout the room. I jumped out of the bed, placing my feet on my black carpet rug as I yawned all the way to the bathroom. I ran hot water over my face towel as I dampened my face and brushed my teeth.

"Good morning baby, *Happy birthday to you!*" Mom and Aunt Jasmine sang in unison.

"I forgot it's my birthday," I stated with my hand over my mouth.

"Well I didn't. No matter how sick I am baby, Mama didn't forget and your aunt has a nice day planned out for you for your special day as soon as you get out of school."

This would definitely be the most memorable birthday of my life and I couldn't wait. My mama actually went to a store in the mall and bought me the cutest pink dress and my aunt curled my hair for me. Chapter 15 was now open in my life but I had to admit that I was a little scared about it. I had to mentally prepare myself about leaving for Georgia and not ever seeing my mother again. I really didn't have much to celebrate but I tried to keep my mind off the bad things.

***

"It's your birthday?" Amauri asked as I walked into the classroom with a few dollars pinned to my shirt.

"Yes, it is," I smiled.

"You didn't tell me," he stated.

"I forgot," I said sadly.

44

He sat back into his desk as the crew reached into their pockets and pulled out twenties and fifties for me to pin on the safety pin.

"Thanks, guys," I smiled as I put my backpack on the floor.

We all began to work on our assignments, but today our teacher decided to pair us with different partners for another media assignment. I moved to another seat with my new partner as Amauri gave me a strange look.

"Charisma Peyton," a student yelled into the classroom as she read from a yellow note.

"Yes?" I asked surprised.

"You're leaving early; your mother has given you permission to walk home."

"Okay," I stated as I grabbed my backpack suddenly and Amauri mouthed the words, *Is everything okay?* I just shrugged my shoulders because I didn't know anything, and my mom didn't believe that I needed a phone just yet, but due to the circumstances, I really wanted to debate with her regarding this.

I walked swiftly to the front door and through the metal detectors, and to my surprise Aunt Jasmine was standing in front of a limo with roses.

"Oh my god!" I screamed in shock as I grabbed ahold of my aunt.

"I knew you would love it," she smiled as the driver standing next to her opened the door for us.

My entire birthday was so special and on point. My aunt informed me that my mother now had a private nurse to help assist her through her final days. She also helped me find the prettiest red dress that hugged my curves right and it wasn't too tight. She bought me a few different eyeliners, eyeshadows and lip gloss. I was excited about going to my first dance and to have my first dance with Amauri. It took my mind off my mother until we made it home and I saw her laying in her bed sound asleep. I took off my shoes and lay next to her in the bed and watched her sleep. It was the first time I noticed Mom without hair. I kissed her bald head as she rolled over, shocked to see me.

"Hey baby," she whispered between breathing.

"Hey Mama," I replied.

"I hope you had a good birthday."

"I did Mama and it's one that I will never forget," I stated as I kissed her cold cheek and hugged her tight.

CHAPTER 5

The Dance...

"Happy Valentine's Day, baby," Mom said as she hugged me. She was staring at me in the mirror as she watched Aunt Jasmine put on my makeup. "Everyone is going to envy you at the dance tonight."

I was so in love with my look and I couldn't wait to see Amauri tonight. We had been back talking on the phone every night up until tonight. I still didn't get the chance to tell Mom that I officially had a boyfriend, but one of her gifts to me was a cell phone that I would be receiving in a few days.

Since my aunt Jasmine was dropping me off, we decided that we would just meet in the front of the Hilton Anatole where the dance was located. I would go inside and wait for her to leave and meet him in the front.

Aunt Jasmine dropped me off and I waited for Amauri to show up. I waited at least fifteen minutes as I walked back inside and asked the desk agent if I could use the phone and I dialed his number. He didn't answer the three times that I tried, so I put the phone down and felt a pain in the pit of my stomach. I felt uneasy, like something wasn't right, but I didn't know what until I saw Dameon and the fellows walking over.

"Hey, you look nice," he stated as he spun me around.

All the fellows seemed to love my new look as they stared at me. "Amauri has something special for you," Alex stated as he spun me around.

"What do you mean? Where is he?" I questioned.

"He actually got some type of fancy dinner at his place set up just for you," Dameon smiled with an evil grin.

"I don't get it," I replied. "What about the dance?"

"Y'all are going to come back to the dance," he answered swiftly.

"There is food inside," I insinuated.

"Yea but both of you can be alone and enjoy each other's company and maybe do something that he will never forget. He told us that you are going to Georgia and he's been sad about that," he explained.

"Really?" I asked as I thought about the possibility of leaving.

"What's wrong? Are you still a little girl? Afraid of being alone with him?" Alex teased.

"I'm not afraid of anything," I replied in a sassy tone.

"Prove it," Dameon stated.

"I don't even know where I'm going," I explained.

"It's a surprise; just trust us and we will take you to Amauri because it's getting late and he wants to spend time with you," he stated as he stared at his gold-diamond incrusted Rolex.

"Follow us," Charles instructed as he walked out the front door with two red balloons with a card attached. I opened the card as we walked and smiled with joy as I read it out loud. *"Happy Valentine's Day—you're something special and I can't wait to see you,"* I jumped into the car as Dameon opened the door to the passenger side and sat behind me. He placed a blindfold over my eyes as Charles began to drive.

"Why are you covering my eyes?" I asked.

"It's the best surprise in the world and we don't want to ruin it," Dameon instructed as he laughed and sped off.

The moment the car stopped was the moment that changed my life forever. I felt someone tug on my arm as they helped me to get out of the car and another one helped me to walk into the house.

"Amauri, are you in here man?" Dameon shouted as an echo serenaded throughout the house.

"Lay her down here," I heard a voice instruct.

"What?" I yelled as I tried to use my hand to remove the bandana, but they were too strong. I was helpless as they threw me on an air mattress and laughed amongst each other. I felt so helpless and they were in control of everything. The worst feeling in the world was to try to fight for my life and Amauri was right there. I trusted him, and I thought these guys were my friends, but most of all I thought Amauri cared about me. Tears dropped from my eyes as I was raped and passed around like I was nothing. I thought I deserved nothing but death after they had their way with me, and I ran all the way home in my ripped dress that practically turned to shreds.

CHAPTER 6

Charisma Lachelle Peyton

"Damn, she is fine as wine," Conner stated softly as I stood in front of him on the elevator. The sweet fragrance of *Tender Love* by Bath & Body works was sending chills up and down his spine. I heard him talking to his friend behind me as I pressed 22 on the elevator.

"Smells just like candy," his friend commented as he leaned in to get a better whiff of my perfume.

"Excuse me," I interrupted their conversation, turning around swiftly. I was real familiar with the human breath on my back or neck and I didn't like it all. I was two seconds away from macing him directly in his face.

"Dude, just step back," Conner suggested to his friend as he backed up slowly and shrugged his shoulders as he stood back next to him.

I grinned as I waited for the elevator to make it to my floor. I couldn't help but to scurry off the floor as I rolled my eyes at Conner's friend. Conner was handsome, nice and chocolate. I liked his almond, bump-free skin and perfect teeth. I had worked for the company now for two years and was introduced to Conner; he was the head of security. I could tell he liked me by the way he looked into my eyes as he asked questions and I answered. He was definitely into me, but I didn't see anything but red because all I wanted was revenge. I didn't have time for anything else because distractions were nothing but an impulse.

I sat at my desk, clocked in and began to place my newest client's document on my computer. I was working for one of the biggest law firms in New York after attending Howard law school. I no longer went by my first name and was now Lachelle, which was my middle name. As I sat at the computer, I moved the bracelet from my wrist that covered the scars that never healed inside. I ran my fingers over the scars as I went in deep thought, thinking about what happened to me and how it still felt like it was yesterday.

Ten years ago, I was raped by guys that I trusted, and they killed me mentally, physically and emotionally. They killed my dreams of going to fashion design school because everything I loved and wanted to do didn't feel right anymore. I can still remember what happened and every time I think about it, all I can do is think about the sweetest revenge.

Back to the past...

"It's strange that she wasn't at the dance," I heard my aunt say loudly as she searched through the house. "CHARISMA!"

I lay in the tub with my arms dangling as a small pool of blood made a puddle on the tile floor. I was fading away slowly as I lay naked in the bathtub. I didn't want to be rescued; I just wanted to die. I felt mutilated. I felt like I was nothing, disgusting and God didn't love me anymore.

"Oh my god!" aunt Jasmine yelled as she tried to pull me out of the tub.

"What's wrong?" I heard my mother ask as she walked in. "Noooooooooooooo!" she yelled as she fell to the floor after staring at my naked body and cut wrists.

Aunt Jasmine grabbed her cell phone from her breast and dialed 911. "Yes, my niece has cut herself and she isn't talking, and I don't know what to do. She just turned 15 and I think she tried to kill herself because her mom is dying from cancer," she explained. "Please come to 1649 Dowdy Lane in the Turtle Creek complex; the gate code inside the community is 91717."

"Please God! Not my baby," Mom cried as she crawled over to my lifeless body.

Things just weren't the same any longer. The ambulance was able to get me to the hospital quickly to save me and wrap my wrists to stop the blood flow. They told my mom and aunt that if I had lost any more blood that I would have possibly died or needed a blood transfusion.

I spent the next three months in a psych ward where I was surrounded by mental patients all day. These teens were schizophrenic or just had different issues, which required all types of different medicine on a daily basis.

Every morning we all stood in line, awaiting our medicine, and as soon as I took mine, I went back into my room and removed it from under my tongue. I never took the medicine because I didn't like the way it made me feel the first time that I took it. So, I found a razor, hid it until I needed it, and made a small cut inside in the mattress to place the pills in. It was a daily routine of mine. I hated to wear the branded white shirt and pants that read *Patient* across the chest. No one was able to visit me and that hurt me to the core. I could make phone calls twice a week and for some reason, one day I made a call to Amauri. He answered the phone so happy, but I stood there holding onto the phone because I was unable to say anything. So, I hung the phone up and walked away.

There was no one who seemed to be normal in the ward. I met someone who was two years older than me named Dion. He was really crazy and would always stare at me and say weird things to me. He sat behind me, smelling my hair and complimenting my skin all the time.

Dion literally freaked me out and the security guards would do absolutely nothing about him sniffing me like I was a dog. Thankfully, one day while I sat in the movie room, I met Kandice, who was a beautiful person, yet was disturbed.

"Get your weird ass out of hair," she yelled to Dion as he moved from behind me quickly.

Instantly, we clicked becoming the best of friends. She scared Dion off and he left me alone for good. We would stay in my room playing cards and talking about what we wanted to do when we grew up.

One day Kandice stormed into my room angry as she stood in

front of me. I didn't know what to do or how to console her.

"I just want to fuck up my grandfather," she stated as she pounded her fist together as tears rolled down her face.

"What happened?" I asked in shock as I plopped down on my hard ass bed.

"Apparently, he was given custody of me and he will be able to pick me up in eighty days," Kandice explained.

"Isn't that good news? You talked about how dirty your family is but if someone else can give you a home then it will be okay, right?"

"My grandfather is the sick bastard that raped me and got me pregnant when I was twelve. My mother took me to the clinic and made me get an abortion and when they were done, she took me home and I had to sit there and eat at the table with my fucked up ass grandfather."

"Did she know it was him Kandice?"

"She didn't allow me to explain. My mother thought so bad about me that she didn't care who did it because she knew I was already fucking my boyfriend."

"I didn't know," I stated as I placed my hand on top of hers to comfort her as tears dropped down my face.

"Everyone in my family hates me. My mother doesn't love me because I am disgusting to her, and when she found out that I was gay, it fueled to the fire. My boyfriend was actually a girl named Kayla and my mom found us kissing when she walked through the door."

"Wow," I replied in a shocked tone.

"It was supposed to be a sleepover with all of my friends. All of my friends had it all and were so popular, and here I was getting fucked by my own grandfather. I hated men after that. He was fingering me when I was ten and started to sex me when I was eleven. I will never forget how he hurt me and made me feel. I can still remember the smell of his Bengay and the tobacco he would chew between pumps. I wanted to throw up in his mouth as he came inside of me and kissed my neck while his sweat dropped on my face. He was every bit of 250 pounds of pure muscle and there was no escaping or telling the world about him."

"Why?" I asked.

"Because he would kill me, and I was scared, but the craziest thing about it is I tried to kill myself by taking forty hydrocodone pills."

"Oh my god."

"I just wanted my mother to love me and I couldn't tell her what was going on, but it really affected me. I will never have kids; the doctors informed my mother at our last doctor appointment and that was when I decided that I'd rather be dead than to be in the same household as my mother and grandfather."

"Wait, you said that you were fucking your boyfriend who was a girl, so how would your mom think that you were pregnant by her?"

"Well, I did have sex with a few boys at the school until I met her. My mom heard so many stories about me being a complete slut with the boys at school and for a month when I was fourteen, she sent me to a girl's home."

"Damn, and I thought I was going through something."

"I was put out of the girl's home as well, so my mother had no clue what to do with me and it wasn't like she cared. She was too busy with her gangsta boyfriend who is using her for her money," she explained. "But, enough about me. We are always talking about me."

"Not much to say."

"So, I can talk my head off and tell you everything in the world about me, but you won't let me in?" she asked as she sat down on the floor in front of me.

"Alright ladies, time to go to bed and time for you to go to your own room," Nurse Jones stated as she opened the door and pointed to Kandice.

"Okay," she replied as she stood up. "We will finish this discussion tomorrow," she added in.

Kandice and I became the best of friends in the short months we were together in the psych ward. I learned a lot about her life and when she became fed up of being raped by her grandfather and having her entire world rocked. She dreamed of owning her own center where she could help young girls to get through what she had been through. Even though she didn't reach her peak where she could finally tell her mom about her grandfather, she was able to tell me and that was a big step and a great load off her shoulders.

No one in the ward knew why we were there personally. The shrinks tried their best to get what they wanted out of us but couldn't, so they just cast us as another one of the crazies inside the ward. I never told a soul about what happened to me and I thought I never would be able to.

I decided to open up to Kandice around the 80th day of our unpleasant stay. We were home schooled from a center inside of the ward and were in a basic computer class one day when we were asked to go to the news website for our city.

I became frozen as I stared at the online article. It was an article with a picture of Amauri, Charles, Alex, Dameon, and Carter. They had a huge article explaining their lives, how they were going to the championships and the colleges that they would all be attending. Tears slowly crept down my face, falling onto the keyboard. It was an indescribable feeling of hatred. I wanted them dead and I wanted them to feel their entire world torn apart.

I stood up from the computer, grabbing my notebook and ran back to my room in a hurry. I guess Kandice saw me emotionally unstable and ran to my defense.

"What's wrong?" she asked as she opened the door.

I couldn't say anything for an hour straight. I stared at the wall as she held my hand. She didn't know what was wrong, but she was the kind of person to be there for someone that she cared about, and I felt like myself to be around her and be able to tell her something that I couldn't even tell my own mother and aunt.

"I want to kill someone," I stated with authority as I stood up and released her hand from mine.

"What?" she asked in astonishment.

"I haven't been honest with you," I replied as I looked into her eyes. "I was raped by five of the star players on the football team."

"Oh my god!" she stated as she tried to console me.

I stepped back as I continued to talk. "I want them all to die. I want them to feel what I felt, but even worse."

"We will get them all," she explained. "Those bastards are going down, one by one."

***

A few days later, Kandice was released into the custody of her grandfather because her mother left town with her boyfriend. Kandice cried as she left with him and I knew from the pits of my soul that she would be back.

I was right, because a few days later, the nurses and police brought her back into the ward strapped onto the bed. I ran out of my room when I heard her screaming and crying as they shoved a needle in her arm to quiet her down.

"What happened?" I asked Kandice as the nurses held me back.

"He did it again, Charisma," she replied as they moved her to *the dungeon*. The dungeon was a dark room without a bed, covers, or sanity. It was cold and lonely. I felt bad for Kandice as I saw them push the stretcher towards the room. I knew they were going to sedate her with heavy drugs until she passed out and woke up in a few days.

A week later Kandice was released and was able to come back into the facility where they placed her in an isolated room. I wasn't able to talk to her for days until they thought it would be okay. I walked into her room as she stared into space. I kept thinking my poor friend was under so many drugs that it truly didn't make any sense. I sat on the floor next to her as she was sitting on the edge of the hard bed. Placing my head on her legs as she began to cry eventually brought tears to my eyes. She was so dingy, smelled like mothballs and her hair was frizzy like she had been electrocuted.

"I killed him," she mumbled as she looked away at the wall to stare into my eyes.

"You killed your grandfather?" I asked in shock.

More tears tumbled down her face as she stood up. "As soon as we made it home, he cooked dinner and it was a nasty tetrazzini with cucumbers sliced on the side. He had our plates at the table as if he was happy to see me home, as if he had done nothing to me." She wiped the snot from her nose with a towel and continued between soft cries as she paced back and forth.

"What happened next?" I asked in an eager tone.

She turned around and faced me. "I didn't eat his nasty ass food and he was offended like normal. He went in the refrigerator, popped open a twelve pack of beer and was drunk within the next thirty minutes. I waited for him to pass out on the couch before I made my way back into my room. I thought I locked the door, Charisma." She continued to cry as she fell to the floor.

"Tell me," I demanded as I wiped away her tears.

"He came in my room after I fell asleep and he tried to touch me. I was sleeping hard I guess because when I woke up he had my legs pried apart and was about to enter me, until I kicked him in his mouth and he choked me. I always kept a knife under my bed and he didn't clean my room, so as I struggled for my last breath, somehow I felt the knife under the pillow and gathered enough strength to stab him in his head."

"Oh my god!" I screamed.

"My hands were covered with blood. It was on the covers, pillows and there was a puddle of blood on the floor." Kandice paused as she took a glance at her hands, still thinking about the moment. "He didn't scream anymore or reach for me. I watched him die and I had no regret about it. I smiled at the fact that I had killed the person who made me this way. I have no one in my family anymore and no one will ever forgive me for what I've done."

Kandice and I talked the rest of the day until it was time for me to go back into my room. I couldn't believe what had happened to Kandice. I felt so bad for her because she was violated just like I was. After her court appearance and petitioning as insane, she would be with the psych ward for the next two years, and they would be sending Kandice to one of the biggest mental institutes in Terrell, Texas. I was saddened to find out that she would be there for the next ten years. I told her no matter what that we would always have a way of communication with each other and we were bonded together like glue. My first tattoo was the last day before they sent her away. Kandice found a razor, sterilized it and we cut our initials into each other's backs very small.

The nurses knew how close we were and allowed me to spend the night in her room. We stayed up practically all night as we painted each other's nails and toes.

"I can't believe they hurt you like that," Kandice blurted out.

"What?" I laughed. "What are you talking about?"

"I know this is random, but do you ever think about getting revenge?"

"Revenge?"

"Yea, do you think about those fucking boys that messed you up?"

"I think about them all the time and I wish they would all drop dead," I assured her.

"Well fucking do it. I'll help you," she explained.

"I couldn't even do something like that and I wouldn't get away with it."

"I have a plan that will take them all down, one by one, but you gotta do it my way and in a couple of years when they think you vanished."

"I'll do it."

Before I could even look up, Kandice had kissed my lips softly. I didn't know if I was supposed to kiss her back or push her away but, surprisingly, I did neither. I just stood there as she kissed me like I was a boy. We fell on the bed, giggling as she continued to kiss me and rub on my breast. My heart was beating rapidly as her hands guided to my private place. I grabbed her hand and threw it off me.

"I'm sorry," she stated.

"I don't think we should be doing this."

"We don't have to. I love you Charisma and I would never hurt you."

"I am not gay," I blurted out.

"I'm sorry, please forgive me," she begged.

"It's okay; let's just never mention it again."

"Okay."

Kandice had the perfect idea to help me with getting revenge on the guys that hurt me. I had so much anger built up inside of me, but I don't think I could ever kill anyone. I couldn't imagine seeing blood or watching someone take their last breath.

"What's your middle name?" Kandice asked randomly.

"Lachelle, why?"

"As soon as you graduate, lose all contact with all family and friends except me. Don't get comfortable with anyone and don't fall in love. When you graduate from college, your new name that people will know will be Lachelle," she informed me.

"You're crazy," I laughed.

"I might be crazy, but I have the biggest plan that will change your life forever. You did say that your mom is loaded, right?"

"She is, but I won't see anything until I am 18," I replied. "I don't even want to think about my mom leaving this world so I could inherit everything."

"I'm sorry; I didn't mean it like that."

I never knew why Kandice asked me those questions. It was extremely weird and it did make me feel uncomfortable.

CHAPTER 7

Back to the Present...

I graduated high school in top 10% of my class with nothing but full scholarships handed to me from different prestigious universities. My mother lived to see me walk across the stage and she beat cancer. I don't know how when they told her that she only had two weeks to live before I tried to commit suicide. I ended up moving to Georgia with aunt Jasmine where she enrolled me into school. I kept to myself, began to study law, and joined the criminal justice team at Peachtree High. I stayed to myself in high school and went to a prestigious college in another state. I hated to keep away from my mom and my aunt.

Kandice and I kept in touch with plans to wreak havoc sooner or later. I took the liberty of studying all the guys. I used fake accounts to find everyone but for some reason, I couldn't find Amauri. I had so many dreams of him and just wanted to know why he did this to me along with his friends.

Different thoughts haunted my mind every night as I slept in my king size bed in my one-bedroom apartment in Harlem, New York. I relocated to New York without any communication with my mother or my aunt. I decided it was perhaps the best choice to take. I had to re-invent who I was and study who I needed to become. Sadly, after making the choice to not communicate with my aunt and mother, my mother passed due to a tumor just two years ago. I guess not being there for her as she died left a big imprint on my heart and hatred in my soul. I was mad at the world, angry with God and all I wanted to do was kill the people who killed me mentally and emotionally. I made my mind up and I definitely wasn't the peon ass, fifteen-year-old girl again. I finally had a voice of my own that no one would ever take from me again. I had gotten a whole new identity: fake I.D., credit cards and a new outlook on life. I was a completely different person and I was no longer the naïve freshman. No one would ever hurt me again.

Time was ticking, and revenge had to be sweet. Ten years had finally passed completely and it was time for the savagery to begin.

"Lachelle, are you okay? You don't seem yourself today," Doctor Agma asked as she lifted my chin with her hand.

"Oh yeah, I'm fine," I replied. "Just thinking about my future and how this new look makes me not only look beautiful, but feel beautiful," I complimented as I gawked into the mirror at myself.

"Everything appears to look so good from your surgery a couple of years ago."

Doctor Agma was my doctor for a couple of years now and she transformed my entire face into a new one that no man could resist. My nose was no longer big and stretched out like Pinocchio. I kept my body intact and my ass had gotten bigger over the years as my hips became wider.

"You look completely different from the person that first walked into my office a few years ago," she explained as she held my chin and pressed a machine against it.

I had been to more than twenty dermatologists to help me get rid of the terrible acne I suffered from and also went to a few plastic surgeons to help me fix my nose. I was lucky when I ran into Doctor Agma as we shared a cab ride home a few years back. She gave me her card and extended an offer that I couldn't possibly refuse. I had inherited enough money from my mother's death so I had plenty of money. I already had come into a lump sum when I turned eighteen so I pretty much had my life planned out.

"I love my look and I thank you Dr. Agma for helping me become exactly what I needed to."

"You're welcome, and I know that we won't see each for a while but if you have any problems or concerns, please let me know," she smiled. "I am only one call away."

"I know," I replied as I grabbed my coat from the chair and placed it on my back.

"Do you want to think about maybe breast implants or butt shots?" she asked.

"Now you know I am good in both departments," I boasted as I held my breast and spun around for her to view my ass.

"Well, you can't blame me for trying," she laughed as she held the door for me to leave.

I took a taxicab home as I looked through important files in my briefcase. I had a deposition that needed to be taken to court the following day, so I needed to get on it as soon as possible.

"You are so beautiful," the cab driver complimented as he stared at me through the rearview mirror.

"Thanks," I replied dryly in deep thought.

"Your melanin is so beautiful. You make an old man wish for younger days," he goofed.

I laughed without a reply as he turned down the street. Traffic was horrible as usual and I knew this ticket was going to be at least $200. I knew why he was smiling bright because he was about to get his coins in tonight with me.

As soon as he pulled up to my apartment, I paid him and searched for my keys inside of my purse to open the door.

"Hey, bitch!" Kandice screamed as she practically jumped on me, almost causing me to tilt over.

"Wow, you look great girl," I replied as I stared at her.

"I guess the crazy house does wonders, yah know?" she laughed as I shook my head in disbelief that she was finally out and free. We talked over the years, plotted our plans strategically, and came together as a force. She was my friend and the only one that I trusted because she was consistent throughout the years.

"You're still a shit talker, I see," I replied while laughing.

CHAPTER 8

Alex Rodriguez: Pain & Pleasure

My first task at hand was the easiest to come. He was the slowest player on the team for the out of country basketball team. They played different teams in New York but mostly overseas. I investigated his likes and dislikes and researched everything about him. He was definitely in for a surprise. I went to one of the biggest balls in the city and he was the host of the night. I walked in with all eyes on me with my red-velvet corset dress on and 40D breast sitting up just right in them. I made sure to make an impression on him as he eyed me as I danced the night away on the dance floor. I swayed my hips to all the slow songs as he encouraged the DJ to play different songs.

"Red dress, got yah boy feeling some type of way," he yelled into the microphone as he looked at me. I pretended not to care as he said different things trying to capture my attention. The women seemed to be jealous as they bumped me, practically bum rushing me for Alex's attention. This was going to be harder than expected. I kept thinking of other ways to get his attention, but he wasn't biting. There were too many women on the floor shaking their asses, twerking hard and being plain thotty.

I decided to take a break from the mess as I walked up to the bar. I ordered a Long Island Iced Tea with ice as I moved my head up and down to the beat.

"Oh my god, your masquerade mask is so beautiful," a young lady complimented as she walked past me.

I smiled as I thanked her. My best friend had picked up a trade inside of the psych ward and was sewing her ass off. She was making dresses, pantsuits and anything you could think of. I told her that she should have been a seamstress for the celebrities.

I felt a body sit next to me and the person was a little too close for comfort. "You got a banging ass body, ma," Alex stated as he stared at me. "It's just something about you."

"Oh, really," I replied dryly.

"I am feeling you ma."

"Feeling me?" I inquired. "You don't even know me." I waved him off as I left a fifty-dollar tip for the bartender and walked away in stride.

"Damn," he stated almost foaming at the mouth as he followed me out the door.

"What do you want from me?" I asked as I pressed the elevator button down. I needed to seem as uninterested as I possibly could. I knew he was the type that couldn't take no for an answer.

"Ma, I just want to get to know you." He extended his hand for me to shake but as I stuck mine out, he took the palm of mine and kissed it.

I almost threw up in my mouth when I thought about everything that happened to me. A mini flashback occurred that made me step back into the elevator.

"I'm Alex Rodriguez and I am one of the highest paid players in the league right now."

"Cocky, aren't we?" I giggled as he pressed the stop button on the elevator as he entered and closed the doors.

"You are playing hard to get but those beautiful eyes are telling me a story that I want to read," he stated as he pulled off my mask. He stared at me for a moment as my heart began to beat rapidly and thump inside my chest. I didn't know what to do and was scared at the thought of him figuring out exactly who I was.

"You're beautiful," he commented as he kissed my lips sensually. I played along and allowed him to kiss me passionately as he held onto my ass. "I want you so bad; damn I love black girls' pussy."

He began to unfasten his designer belt and threw it on the floor. I didn't know what to do at this point. I couldn't do anything to him here on this elevator because I was the last person seen with him as he followed behind me on the elevator.

"Hold up," I replied, trying to catch my breath. "Why don't we get a room or go back to my place or something. I am not going to fuck you in this elevator," I mentioned as I fixed my dress and pressed the start button on the elevator.

"Okay ma, how about you meet me at my condo; it's right down the street."

"Give me the address," I demanded.

He put the address in my GPS on my phone as the elevator doors opened and he walked me to my car. I was shitting bricks thinking about what was going to happen and if I could even go through with this.

"I look forward to seeing you," he stated with warmth as he kissed my palm again while holding the door for me to get inside my car.

"Likewise," I lied as I tried to smile. "Do you think there were any cameras on that elevator?" I asked.

"No, I'm positive. I looked around and scoped it out while we were on it," he assured me.

"Great."

"Don't stand me up, baby," he mentioned as he walked away to jump inside of his limo.

The GPS stated that it would take fifteen minutes before I arrived, so I called Kandice and placed my phone on the holder as I spoke with her on the car system.

"The plan is in motion," I stated before she could speak.

"Send me your location," she demanded.

"Huh?" I asked in shock.

"I know that I didn't mention this in the plan, but I need to be close by because we don't know how strong he is and if the plan will run smoothly. I will be the look-out and I will find a way inside."

"Okay, I just sent you the address."

"Bet," she replied as she hung up the phone quickly.

Kandice was really scaring me. *When did she get all military and shit with all these plans and making up codes?* I thought to myself as I pulled up to Alex's condo. I parked further down the street and walked up to his condo and pressed the doorbell.

"The lovely lady didn't stand me up." He smiled as he jumped behind me and I held my chest.

"You scared the shit out of me," I replied as I punched his shoulder.

"I'm sorry, please forgive me."

"All is forgiven," I stated as I took the bouquet of roses from his hands.

Alex took his keys out of his pocket and opened the door to his condo. The condo was nice as hell with all-white furniture and the view was impeccable. He was living the dream and I was about to be his worst nightmare.

"Drink?" he asked as he walked into his own bar.

"Long Island Iced Tea, please?"

I grabbed the picture that was turned upside down on the bar. My eyes grew big as I looked at the picture over and over again. It was a picture of Karen, my former friend from high school, and Alex with three kids.

Alex turned around after I didn't answer his question because I was in deep thought. I had gotten completely quiet. He snapped his fingers to get my attention.

"Are you okay?" he asked as he took the picture frame away from me and placed it back on the bar, face down.

"I'm okay," I lied. "I just was feeling a little light headed I guess."

"Well, do you need aspirin or anything?" he asked with concern.

"Yes, that would be perfect and a little music so I can unwind."

"I got exactly what you need baby," he mentioned as he walked to the back.

I pulled two pills out of my purse that would make him drowsy and dizzy. I opened each capsule and poured them into his beer as I placed the empty capsules right back into my purse.

"Here you go," he stated. "Sorry it took so long." I looked at the pill and this dummy was trying to fucking rape me. It wasn't an aspirin; it was the date rape pill. I studied all the different pills and codes on pills in college, so I knew what this fucked up ass man was going to try to do to me. I pretended that I took the pill as I sipped my tea and he chugged his beer like it was no tomorrow.

"You don't wear your ring?" I asked as I stared at his empty finger.

"I'm going through a divorce," he responded dryly.

"She seems nice from the pictures and you have a nice-looking family," I complimented.

"Thanks," he laughed.

"What's funny?" I asked.

"My wife and I were high school sweethearts, but I never wanted her fat ass. It was just one of those things where my dad made me fucking marry her, after she threatened to put me on child support in high school. I gave the bitch the money to have an abortion and what did she do? She kept the money and didn't get rid of the baby. Years after I just kept having more kids, but I never loved her, and we are finally getting a divorce." Alex was becoming belligerent at this point as stood his cocky ass up and tried to kiss me. "She knew I was getting a deal and no one was going to give me a deal when I already had baby mama drama coming into the league."

I decided to tease him a little. "Go lay down on the bed and get butt naked. I'm about to suck your dick like it's no tomorrow." He smiled with a big grin as he staggered to the room and I pulled my phone out my purse to text Kandice.

Me: Come upstairs now. I'm about to unlock the door, the drug is already in his system.

Kandice: Bet.

I opened the door waiting on Kandice to come inside and she hid in the kitchen. "Baby, where are you at?" he yelled through the room.

"I'm coming baby, just getting ready for you," I explained as I pulled my dress over my head, exposing my velvet red see-through lingerie.

"Damn, he already calling you baby," Kandice whispered as she laughed quietly.

"Shut up," I whispered.

I walked into the bedroom slowly as he lay on the bed, stroking his red penis. It was gross and small looking. I jumped on top of him and kissed him passionately as I removed his hand from his dick and began to stroke him myself.

"Ohhh yeah baby, just like that," he groaned as I continued and he nutted in two minutes. "Are you going to take off these black and red mittens that you're wearing?"

"Oh no, these are my good luck mittens."

"Oh okay," he replied.

"You already done," I stated.

"No, just give me a couple of minutes and I want that super wet, pretty black pussy," he stuttered.

I stood up as he stared at me. I noticed the radio and turned it on and R. Kelly's "Seems Like You're Ready" was playing. I began to dance slowly to the beat and sing to the lyrics of the song as he watched me, practically asleep.

"I bet you miss this pussy, right," I stated as I crawled on the bed to stroke his now hardened dick again. "You want this pussy again," I teased. "You want to feel what I felt," I asked as Kandice walked inside the room and passed me a scalpel.

"What are you talking about? I can't miss something that I never had."

Alex was moaning until he felt the tip of his dick after I cut it off. "Omg," he yelled as he stood up, holding his bloody dick.

"Do you feel the warmth now? Does the oozing feel like my juices?" I asked as I laughed, watching him holler as he held his dick with pain. "Tie him up, Kandice."

Kandice walked over quickly and hit him in the head with a pistol as she tied him onto the chair. "He's fucking bleeding everywhere," she stated as she tied his hands tightly.

"Place a towel over his scrawny dick." I demanded as she grabbed a towel from the bathroom. We waited for him to wake up about an hour later and he could barely open his eyes. He seemed weak and completely out of it.

"Why are you doing this me?" he asked with a tear falling down his face. "What did I do you?" he mumbled as his lifeless body lay in the chair.

"Ten years ago, you killed me," I stated as I walked over to stand in front of him. "I was once a young girl, who had a future and wanted to just be a normal girl. I had to watch my mama suffer and then I had to fucking suffer because the popular football players tricked me for one night of your sick pleasure."

His eyes were open at this point, wide as he stared into my eyes. "Charisma," he stated in a surprising tone.

"Not anymore, you killed her," I stated with clarity. "It's Lachelle now."

"I never forgot about you," he stated.

"You're sick and I bet you never had any remorse for what the hell you did to me."

He talked with pain in his voice and I knew he was slipping away. "All the years and I thought I would never see you again," he stated. "Look in the third drawer under my clothes," he coughed so hard that blood was now coming out of his mouth.

"No, I'll look," Kandice stated as she walked over to the dresser. "There is no telling what this stupid guy is trying to do."

Kandice slid the dresser door open and pulled all of the clothes out of the drawer. "There is nothing here, you little dick," she stated in anger as she continued to search the drawers.

"Pull the board of the dresser out," he yelled with his head down as blood spit out of his mouth like a faucet.

"Panties?" Kandice asked with the panties in her hands.

I turned around and stared at them as I fell to the floor. It was the panties that Alex stuffed into his front pocket before he raped me for the second time.

"What's wrong?" Kandice asked as she tried to follow the expressions on my face.

"You mutherfucker!" I yelled as I stood up and pried the underwear from Kandice hands. I ran close to him and practically put them in his mouth, stuffing it as he cringed and yelled.

"What is going on?" Kandice asked confused.

"Those were the fucking panties that I wore that night."

"Wow, are you sure?"

"I am very sure," I pleaded. "I remember this shit like it was yesterday."

"Okay," Kandice said silently as she pulled the pistol from the back of her pants and shot him one time in the head. He slumped over in the seat, castrated with blood all over. "Sorry, I just can't stand to see my best friend hurting."

I stood there shaken up as I stared at his dead body. I could smell the smoke from the gun, but I couldn't move.

"Go put your dress back on and get all your belongings, throw the Trackphone in the dumpster and wait for me in your car until you see me pull off."

"What? Why?"

"I need to wipe down everything and I don't need you in the way."

I waited ten minutes for Kandice to take care of everything and as soon I watched her hop off into her car, I followed right behind her. I felt so liberated and in control of my life as I sped behind her. So many men were getting away with raping women or sexually abusing them, but I knew at least five that would never be a threat to any more women. I vowed that each one of them would all die the most horrific death that anyone could mastermind. Now, the plan was in motion for Carter who was next up. The rest of the men may not be so easy to try to get into bed with, especially if they are as happily married as some of them pretended to be on Facebook. I called it Fakebook because everyone pretended to be everything they wished they could be. Carter was exactly that; he was playing for the Nets until he broke his leg in three places in a skiing incident. It appeared he was never the same after from social media.

CHAPTER 9

Carter Strong

One month later...

"Hello, I'm here to apply for the customer service representative job at Aretok," I inquired as I took the clip from the desk and spoke with the front desk receptionist.

"Really? We've never had anyone know what company they wanted to work for," the front desk receptionist stated with a smile as she took a glance at my *Dior* purse.

"That is so cute," she complimented.

"Oh thanks, it was on sale," I replied. "Karen is it?"

"How did you know?" she asked in shock.

"Wild guess," I responded as I pointed to her badge. It was strange that she was working at the very place that I needed to be hired at. Maybe Alex had asked Carter to give her a job since he claimed that they were divorcing. I could tell she had no clue at all who I was, so I kept giving her compliments as she continued to talk. "I saw an ad in the paper and I felt that I was extremely qualified for the position."

"Your resume looks impeccable," she complimented as she looked over my resume.

"Thanks," I smiled.

"If you have time, I would like to interview you for the position with Aretok through our temporary agency and believe it or not, most of our temps have successfully made it full time with our companies after sixty days."

"I am so excited and I look forward to longevity with the company." We both conversed as she showed me the way to the conference room. She was sold on my compliments and my conversation. Karen was definitely putty in my hands.

A week later...

"I hope your first day is pleasant," Karen said before she hung up the phone.

My interview through the temporary agency went well. I was hired on the spot by Karen and today was going to be my first day at work. Instead of the customer service position, Karen felt that I would fill the secretary position with greatness because I killed the interview. But, how could I not?

I received all of the details needed for my first day in my new assignment. It was hard playing two different people in my completely difficult life. I had to juggle being an attorney at a firm and working this stupid ass secretary job. I had to do what I had to do to make them suffer.

I walked into the office wearing black red bottoms and a black pants suit with my hair down. I was no longer natural and took a dive into the *crack*. My hair was long, past my shoulders and only a few inches away from my ass. Everyone looked around as the security guard showed me the way to my desk.

"So, you are the new secretary?" the security guard asked as he watched me walk around the desk and licked his lips with approval with his eyes staring at my ass.

"I am," I smiled with content.

"Well, the boss man is always late and the lady that will be training you will be here in about an hour. She left a script for you to say when answering the phones and she also left a sheet of the rules and regulations, Ms. Lady."

"Thanks," I replied.

He wasn't playing at all about Carter being late. I was drained and the day was damn near over when he walked into the office smiling bright, talking into his earpiece. I spoke and he walked right past me as if I was nothing. Carter's office was directly behind me but I had a desk and no doors at all to close.

An hour later, Carter came out to finally greet me. "I am so sorry about that rude first impression of me. I was on a business conference call with my lead administrator and business partners in which you will meet sooner or later. I saw your resume that the agency sent over and I was deeply impressed. I hope you do a good job and decide to stick around."

"Stick around?" I inquired.

"I'm sorry and I don't know if the agency spoke with you about the past employees but they seem to always quit and I told Karla that I needed someone who is dependable and reliable. So, I hope you came to work and make my job a little easier," he retorted as he walked back into his office.

This is going to be tough, I thought to myself as I typed up the weekly memos that he placed on my desk before he walked away.

Later on the same night...

"How was the first day?" Kandice asked as she smiled bright.

"Terrible," I replied as I plopped down on the couch and sighed as I kicked off my heels.

"Why? What happened?" she inquired.

"Nothing, that's the fucking problem," I replied in a discouraging tone. "I don't think I want to do this shit anymore."

"What the hell do you mean? These fuckers violated you and took your fucking life; you better stop bitching up and kill their asses one by one," Kandice screamed angrily.

"I know what the fuck they did to me and I am not bitching up at all. I just want this shit to be over and I am so tired of studying these fools," I cried. "He wasn't biting today and he was rude as fuck."

"What does the fucker like?" Kandice asked with her hands on her hips.

"Hell, I don't know, football I guess."

"That's what you need to use."

"I don't play football, dummy."

Kandice held her side as she laughed continuously. "Girl, I am not talking about playing no damn football. All you need to do is research his games and learn about his likes and dislikes."

"You're so right," I acknowledged as I took my laptop out my bag and began my search on *Google*.

A week later...

I put my deposition away that I was working on and decided to put my soul and heart into studying Mr. Carter Strong.

"Thanks for ordering my lunch, it was great today," Carter stated as he walked out of his office licking his fingers. "I love Odom's Barbeque and that took me home. It's my favorite."

"I'm glad you enjoyed your lunch, sir."

"I'm getting out of here a little early today. The game is coming on and I need to get my house set for my guest."

"Oh okay, so you go all out for game nights?" I inquired.

"I love football," he explained. "It's like the air I breathe; I can't live without it." He grabbed his coat from the coat rack and put it on.

"Wow, I am a big fan myself."

"Oh, really," he stated, surprised, as he turned around.

"I am as a matter of fact," I goofed. "I am actually a big fan."

"Really?" he smiled as he walked back over to my desk. "I have to admit that you surely don't seem like the type to watch football or know anything about it."

"On December 9, 2012, Mr. Strong you returned a punt 88 yards for a touchdown in a home game against the Kansas City Chiefs, making you the oldest player in NFL history to score a touchdown on a punt return."

"Wow! Are you kidding me?" he chuckled with surprise.

"You set the set Raiders franchise records for receptions, receiving yards, and punt return yards," I replied. "You were the best thing going for the Raiders until..."

"Until I hurt my damn leg going on a damn skiing trip," he interrupted.

"It's okay, you were the man and you still are the man."

"I wouldn't say that I was the best of anything," he replied.

"I beg to differ," I smiled. "You had 100 touchdowns, 14,987 receiving yards, 13.7 yards per reception and 1,094 receptions."

"Little lady, you have stunned me today. I think I might have the best secretary in the world," he boasted. "Usually I don't do this, but I would love for you to come over and watch the game with us tonight."

"Really?" I asked in shock.

"It's 2 p.m. now so why don't you go ahead and close up the office today?" he suggested.

"Why not?" I smiled as I shrugged my shoulders and logged out of the computer. Carter wrote down his address and I scurried home to change into something more appropriate. I put on my sexiest red dress that hugged my curves just right. I dashed my lips with *Paint the City Red* which was a very beautiful, dark red color from the cosmetic line: *Coloured Raine.*

"If looks could kill," Kandice laughed as she watched me curl my hair in the mirror.

"I'm going to seduce his ass at his own party," I goofed.

"I know you not going to kill him in front of a lot of people," she inquired.

"Hell no, why you think I didn't invite your ass?" I spat as I turned the light switch off in the bathroom and grabbed my purse and keys from the table.

"I was wondering why you didn't and what was going on."

"I just want to take a new approach with Carter. I want to get to know him and figure out his strengths and weaknesses. I want to play with his mind and make him fall head over heels with me, then as soon as he thinks that he scored the perfect woman, I want to kill him in the most painful way. But first, I want to know exactly why they did this to me."

"You may never get that answer. Just kill all those mutherfuckers and keep it moving after," Kandice blurted out as she turned on the news.

"Sadly, we report that Alex Rodriquez from the Nomad overseas basketball team was found dead today after he was reported missing for three weeks when he didn't board his flight with the rest of the team. The condo manager reported that Alex's car hadn't moved in weeks and received several violations," the reporter stated into the camera as she

walked across the street and gave the mic to an older black man.

"I just knew something was going on because he loves to party and has those wild parties and I told him to slow it down. I tried to have my daily talks with him but he just doesn't listen to me at all. He messes with so many different women that I don't know who it could have been. The poor man was mutilated and I never in my life saw anything like that before. Whoever did that, they don't have a soul or any type of moral compass and I hope they find you," the building manager stated as he walked away crying.

"Oh, boo-hoo mutherfucker," Kandice snarled as she changed the channel to the television. "Fuck his ass girl and don't be in your feelings about the shit either."

"I'm not," I explained. "I have no pity left for any of them mutherfuckers."

"You better not," she stated. "They tricked you just to rape you like you were nothing and now they want to sit around here and pretend to be victims."

I closed the door and locked it. I knew she was right and I was about to play this game with a full deck.

"Taxi!" I screamed as I whistled in the air to the moving taxicab.

"Where to?" the taxi driver asked as I closed the door.

"113 Lenox Avenue," I replied.

"Must be a fancy place that you're headed to," he mumbled as he placed the address in the GPS system.

"Just take me to the address please," I blurted out rudely.

"You women these days are so mean," he stated as he turned the corner.

"I'm sorry; I'm just in a hurry that's all."

"Well, you jumped into the right cab. I promise that I will get you there in no time."

He was right because fifteen minutes later he pulled up to the estate of Carter Strong. I stared at the huge ass mansion and couldn't believe my eyes. I reached into my pocket to pay the driver as I opened the door. I walked up to the gate and pressed zero for the operator.

"Strong Estate. What's your name?" the lady asked on the intercom.

"It's Lachelle," I replied as I bent down to speak into the intercom.

"Lachelle Peyton?" she asked.

"Umm, yes," I answered.

The gate opened and she advised me to walk through the gate to the front of the mansion. I had never seen anything like it at all. Carter's home was something out of a movie and I was mesmerized as I walked past the fountain in the front with fish swimming around it.

There were plenty of cars outside of the mansion and as I walked closer, I could hear the men screaming and yelling at the game.

"The woman of the hour," Carter stated as he opened the door for me to come in. "Please come in. I can't wait to introduce you to everyone."

"Aww, thank you," I replied.

Carter could dress his ass off and he was a handsome man without any kids. It made me wonder just why he did what he did to me ten years ago. I sat by him the entire night as he mingled with guests and walked over to me. He sat right next to me on the couch and I tried my best to flirt. He was un-reactive to any of my approaches and I knew I was the shit.

The game was almost over and Carter had been gone for at least ten minutes. I walked into the kitchen and was taken back by what I had seen. Carter and his so-called best friend were holding hands as they continued to converse. I stood back and hid where they couldn't see me as I peeked from around the corner.

"I see your guest has been flirting with you all night," his handsome friend stated while laughing.

"I guess I still got it," he replied bashfully as he grabbed his homeboy's dick and sucked on his neck like he was a vampire.

I was completely shocked and surprised as I walked back to the living room to sit down on the couch. They came back out shortly with beers in their hands as they smiled at each other for the remainder of the night.

Later on that night...

I opened the door and couldn't even get into the door good because Kandice was waiting. "Damn girl, you at the door like the mailman with W2s," I chuckled.

"You had me scared for a minute," she replied with her hands on her hips. "I text you."

"I know but I was in my thinking zone and he didn't bite for shit."

"Girl, it must be something wrong with him then, especially if he didn't bite."

"His ass is gay," I blurted out.

"Gay?" she inquired.

"Gay as a mutherfucker," I chuckled. "I saw him grab his best friend's dick in the kitchen and he kissed him as he sucked on his neck."

"Wow!" she laughed. "So, this nigga raped you and now his ass is gay?"

"Yeap."

"I have a Plan B for this mutherfucker then."

"Okay, just tell me what I need to do."

Two weeks later...

"You know, you have been doing a magnificent job and I would love to hire you on full time with a raise," Carter explained as he walked out of his office to greet me.

"Wow," I stated as I put my bags down. "The day hasn't even started yet and I got a raise."

"I just feel such a great connection with you and I would love to have you around."

"Thank you so much and you won't regret it. How about I order your favorite for lunch today? It's been a while since you've licked your fingers from the scrumptiousness," I teased.

"You know what? It's Friday and I need a little southern barbeque in my life," he smiled.

"Great, I will order it online when they open."

"Just use my card to pay for it and you might as well order dinner too because it's going to be a long day for you and I."

"Oh yeah, I forgot about audits," I remembered.

I ordered the food online and completed all of my tasks that were assigned to me. Kandice began to text me as the food arrived and I put it on a plate.

Me: The plan is in motion.

Kandice: Bet. I'll make the call in 40 minutes. Make sure he enjoys his lunch.

Me: Bon Appétit MF!!!

"Here's your grub." I opened his office door and placed the food on his desk with a can of Coke and plenty of napkins.

"The ribs smell absolutely delicious," he complimented as he took a huge bite out of one of them. "The barbeque sauce is sweet and tangy today," he noticed.

"Must be a new cook," I stated.

"Yea but it's still good though."

40 minutes later...

"Hey boss, there's a call for you on line one," I yelled.

"Okay, I got it." I could see him rubbing his stomach in pain as he placed the phone onto his ear. He slammed it down hard as he ran out of his office.

"What's wrong, boss?" I asked, pretending like I didn't know anything.

"Damn security company called me; some fool just tried to break into my house so I'll be back."

"Oh no, that's terrible."

"I know, if it's not one things it's another, but I'll be back."

"Okay, I hope everything checks out just fine."

"Me too, cancel that 2 o'clock meeting for me as well," he demanded as he walked out of the office.

I put on my gloves and darted out of the building quickly as I searched around to make sure he didn't see me.

"Fuck!!" he yelled as he looked at his low tire.

"Do you need a ride, sir?" a taxi cab driver asked.

"Just in the knick of time," he gasped. "I will deal with my Bentley later."

I watched as he scurried away in the taxi. I called for the one parked across the street and he took me Carter's address. "Just drop me off here," I told the driver as I paid him and walked from across the street.

I saw that the cab was parked in the front so I walked down the long trail until I reached the entrance. I made sure my gloves were on tight before I opened the door. My heart was beating fast as I walked down the hall to the living room.

"About fucking time," Kandice yelled as she slapped the back of his head. "He's been throwing up and shit," she complained.

Kandice had him tied up to a chair as throw up came out of his mouth, causing the sock to fall out of his mouth. It smelled horrible and I almost threw up as I looked at his defenseless ass continue to throw up on himself. He was throwing up so hard that blood was coming from his nose and mouth.

"Why the fuck is you doing this?" he asked as he stared at me. I could tell the rat poisoning was making him sicker and sicker by the minute.

"Well first, let me tell you what is going to happen to you," I smiled as I walked closer to him. "You see today I poisoned your lunch with rat poison. The poison normally causes bleeding several days after ingestion but I added a few drops of something special to give it the boost it needs. You're going to hemorrhage soon which is going to cause cardiopulmonary effects to your heart and weaken the muscles of your heart as it makes irregular heartbeats. After this is done, it's going to send your body into convulsions and shock."

"Please don't do this," he begged and pleaded.

"It's already been done," I stated calmly as I sat down next to him.

"So, this is the infamous Carter Strong?" Kandice asked as she spat on his face.

"Why the fuck is you doing this?" he asked. "Look I have a safe in my room behind the picture."

"I don't want your money you fucking asshole," I replied snippily. "I want my life back. I want what you and the rest of your shitty ass homeboys took from me," I screamed.

"What the hell are you talking about lady?" he asked with a confused tone as blood poured out of his nose.

"You forgot already?" I asked. "Let me take you back to the past," I turned around as I stripped out of my clothes and took out the red dress. It was the first time that I'd worn it in ten years and I felt a tear about to escape as I turned around for him to see. "The night I wore this was supposed to be the best night of my life but you and your crew decided to rape me. You disgusting fucks took me to an abandoned house and raped me."

"Oh my god!" he cried. "Please forgive me. I didn't rape you at all. They made me hold your arms and they made me be quiet about it after you disappeared."

"I don't give a damn!" I screamed. "You sat there and held my arms because you were scared of not being popular anymore. Did you know that your ass was gay back then as well? So you were trying to hide your gayness and let them rape me to keep your masculinity with them?" I questioned as I slapped his cheek.

He didn't reply. "Tell me mutherfucker! Why did you do this?"

"I've thought about you for years and I prayed to God—"

"God, mutherfucker don't bring your fake God into our conversation," I interrupted as I grabbed a machete from my bag.

"This wasn't a part of the plan," Kandice stated as she stared at me.

"Joy won't feel good if he can't feel more pain," I replied as I walked behind him. "I know he's tied up but I need you to hold him."

"What?" he yelled. "Please don't do this."

Kandice held his weak body as he tried to squirm out of the seat but he didn't have any strength from the poison. She smiled as she watched me cut off one of his hands as he screamed until he passed out. Blood was plastered all over the floor, chair, and my clothes as I cut the other hand. There was so much blood that it caused puddles on the floor. I checked his pulse and he was dead. He wasn't breathing anymore and had no pulse left.

"Mutherfucker," I yelled as I kicked his lifeless body.

"Come on, let's get out of here," Kandice stated as she grabbed me by my arm.

Kandice drove the taxi back to an underground garage 40 miles away and we jumped into her car. No words were said as we bounced our heads to the radio station playing an old school jam of the day: "Many Men" by 50 Cent.

Sunny days wouldn't be special, if it wasn't for rain

Joy wouldn't feel so good, if it wasn't for pain

Death gotta be easy, 'cause life is hard

It'll leave you physically, mentally, and emotionally scarred

We both sang along to the beat as she drove us home. Revenge felt so sweet and I couldn't wait to study my next victim. I wanted revenge in the worst way with this mutherfucker because he was one of the most heartless ones. I smiled at my own deep thoughts on our way home because it was about to grimy.

CHAPTER 10

Dameon Garner: Never Trust a Big Booty and a Smile...

One month later...

Dameon Garner was the boldest motherfucker of all the boys in high school. He was the first one who came to me at the dance, playing on my naïve heart. He knew I was a good girl and I knew he was the mastermind behind everything. I remembered how mean he was in class to me when I wouldn't give him the time of day. I remembered how he tried to touch me in gym and I moved to the other side of the gym. He made me feel so damn uncomfortable.

Surprisingly, he was still in Dallas so Kandice and I took a flight because the killings had the state of New York in a ruckus. The NYPD had no clue of the various murders and no eye-witnesses as well, so we were good and had nothing to worry about.

"Are you ready to come home where it all began?" Kandice asked as we sat on the plane.

"I'm not ready but I know I have to get ready," I replied as I scrolled up and down Dameon's Facebook. He was a true playboy and grew up to be a thugged out Dallas wannabe rapper. He was local with dreams of making it big, past Dallas streets and he promoted his wack ass album like it was no tomorrow.

As soon as the plane landed, we caught a taxi to my house. I made sure that someone checked on it for me and that the taxes were still paid and up to date. Chills were running down my spine as the driver turned downed the street.

"What's wrong?" Kandice asked as she grabbed my hand.

I was practically shaking and trembling at this point. "The last time that I can remember being here was when I cut myself," I stated as I took a glance at my wrists. The tattoos over them couldn't take away the pain as I began to scratch the scars and they began to bleed.

"Stop it now, don't do this," Kandice stated as she ripped her shirt and tied the piece around my wrist.

The taxi driver looked through his rearview mirror and he seemed scared as he pulled up. "Just go please," he stated as we tried to give him the money. He waved us off and made skids in the streets because of how fast he took off.

I was completely embarrassed as Kandice walked to the front door with me. I grabbed the keys from my purse and took a solid deep breathe before I entered the house. I walked through with Kandice walking directly behind me. The house still looked the same and the furniture was in the same place as it was ten years ago. I opened the door to my room and plopped on the bed as I thought about that night and I became more and more enraged. I wanted blood and I wanted Dameon to feel exactly what I felt.

"How do you want to play this one?" Kandice asked as she sat next to me.

"I'm going shopping in the morning for the sexiest, un-classiest dress to get his attention. I saw his Facebook and I know exactly what type of woman he wants. He's fine, a thug, a drug dealer and he is having an album listening party," I explained.

"What's going to make you stand out? I mean you're a bad ass bitch, no doubt, but what is going to make you stand out against the crowd?" she inquired.

"The fact that they haven't seen me before; I am a new face. I know Dallas hasn't changed much since I left and one thing I can remember, like you should, is that they guys always want something new."

"I can agree with you there," she laughed. "These hoes are out of pocket especially when you walk through the door."

"And my eyes are on the prize," I stated laughing as I rubbed my hands together like Birdman.

The next day...

Kandice and I rented a Bentley to cruise the Dallas streets. I wanted to make sure that we were the shit and would make this Dallas trip a weekend to fucking remember. After a day of shopping, we both found seductive dresses to make mouths water. Kandice surprised me because under her baggy clothes, just like me, she had a nice ass shape.

She had been hiding it for the longest and she had always been a pretty girl. She just wasn't much of a person to dress up but she had me as a best friend to help her in that department.

I had forgotten the back roads to my house and my phone died as we tried to make it back to the house.

"Damn, my fucking phone died!" I yelled as I threw it in the backseat.

"Shit and I left mine at your house."

"I think I kind of remember the streets a little," I remembered as I turned down a street.

Instantly as I turned down the street, I had a flashback of me running from the house on the corner. It was the house that I was raped in. I stopped the car in the middle of the street and jumped out of it to walk towards the house just to be sure, and I was correct. I held my head in anguish as I screamed, totally losing it at this point. Everything came back to me so quickly that I could barely get a grip. I could feel them inside of me. I could feel my heart beating as I felt their sweat dripping from their pores onto my body, and the smell of some of them disgusted me. I was ruined after they raped me and I could never forget what they had done to me. I was left physically, mentally and emotionally scarred.

"What's going on?" Kandice asked as she took off her seatbelt and followed behind me.

"Mutherfuckers!" I cried as I walked closer to the house where the roof was now sinking in.

"Tell me what's going on," Kandice stated as she shook me.

"This is the house where they raped me. Everything just came to me as we passed through here; it brought it all back. I just want this to be over and I want to live a normal life and I want to be okay after this. Will this be over?"

"I don't know," Kandice hugged me as we turned around to go back inside of the car. She got in on the driver's side to drive so I could gather my thoughts together.

"No matter what, Dameon is going down tonight and I want to be on a plane getting out of Dallas tomorrow night."

"You know I'm down sis and that's just it," she replied as she turned down a few streets. We finally made it to the house and I poured a glass of Long Island Iced Tea that I purchased from the liquor store after we shopped for new outfits.

"Beam me up, Scottie," Kandice goofed as she held her glass. I remained silent as she turned on the radio and tried to shake her offbeat ass to Anaconda. "Come on and dance with me girl, lighten up."

"I don't feel like it," I replied as I sat down on the chair in the kitchen and rubbed my finger across the dust on the marble tile.

"Look, after these mutherfuckers pay for everything they did to us we are going on a vacation for a while. We need our toes curling in the sand, clear blue water, frozen margaritas and hell, I need some dick."

"What?" I spit out my drink in shock.

"Why are you shocked? I mean I am a woman and I do have needs," Kandice assured me.

"I didn't know you liked men."

"Well, I do," she snapped. "That shit that happened with my grandfather was sick as fuck and it made me gay for a while, but while I was in that fucking mental institution I met someone."

"You met someone?" My eyes grew big as she kept talking and I couldn't believe what I was hearing.

"I still like girls and shit but I fell for someone that really showed me that I was beautiful and not only did he show me, he convinced the people to let me go on time because they wanted to keep my ass longer."

"So, how did you date him inside of there? I mean two crazy people together in a mental place is absurd."

"That's the thing, he wasn't a patient."

"Huh?"

"You heard me, bitch," she boasted. "He was an employee there. He was doing security or some shit straight out of high school because he was ran over or some shit. He said it was a hit and run like they were trying to kill him. Fucked up his dreams of ever going pro but he got a job as a real police man now."

"You fucked him?" I asked boldly.

"Of course, I did," she replied candidly. "My intention was to make him fall for me and bust out of the fucking looney-bin, but he stole my heart."

"Wow and as your best friend I am so mad at you right now."

"Why?"

"I'm supposed to know everything about you and you kept a big secret from me."

"I was going to tell you but we've been so busy. He's moving to New York in a couple of weeks. He came up there a few weeks back to a job interview for NYPD and I want you to meet him when he comes."

"Of course," I said dryly.

"Please don't tell me that you're in your feelings about this."

"I'm not in my feelings about this at all; it's your pussy," I proclaimed.

"Girl, fuck you," she laughed as she hugged me tightly. "I promise that you're going to like him. He's sweet, handsome, talks with sense and for the first time in my life I was made love to, and I can't stop thinking about him. I think I found the one that I could spend the rest of my life with."

"Damn and here I am pining away after these mutherfuckers who raped me and you're in love." I stood up from the seat. "Why don't we just dead this shit? I mean I am very successful and I'm making good money and on top of that my bank account has nothing but zeros."

"You want to call this shit quits because I got some dick? Are you fucking kidding me?"

"Yes, about calling this shit quits and no I'm not kidding you," I spazzed. "You have a life and now you got a man that you're in love with. I have no one and I haven't been on one date or even had sex since the rape. I don't know what love feels like. I don't know who I am anymore; it's like everything is a fucking blur. Is this shit even worth it anymore?"

"Stop thinking crazy. I promise after we kill all of those mutherfuckers that we will be okay and you can have fun," she explained. "Your life is going to be golden after this and hell, we will even get you some good dick."

"Shut up, hoe!" I chuckled.

"Oh, very funny but I want you to be okay after this. Trust me, all those mutherfuckers are going to pay and we aren't giving up until each and every one of them is dead."

"Okay."

Later on that night...

Kandice and I walked into the hotel conference room where the album release party was held, looking like money. We checked into a room inside of the hotel and made our way to the party after we went inside of our room. Everyone stared at us and all the bitches were mugging. The key of the night was to look good and be fucking untouchable. We felt like gods in the building as we sashayed across the dance floor. My big booty was poking out of my tight Lisa Raye dress. We both decided against red when we saw the memo that it was an all-white affair. I'm actually glad we wore white dresses instead that showed off our curvy figures that I used to love to cover up in high school.

We danced the night away as all different types of men came to the dance floor and tried to dance with us. We made sure to keep our bourgeois hats on because we needed to make it seem like one could get us.

I walked over to the bar and Kandice soon followed me as we ordered a glass of wine. "So that's how y'all do?" Dameon asked as he walked up to us.

"Excuse me?" I asked as I sipped my wine.

"Y'all just bring both of y'all fine asses in here and take over my album release party," he acknowledged as he stared us both down.

"Well, we sure didn't mean to do that," I stated as I bit my lip seductively.

"Damn," he hissed. "Where are you ladies from? I know both of y'all are not from Dallas. I've never seen y'all around here before."

"New York," Kandice interjected.

"New York, huh?" he stated as he stared us both up and down. "Thick like a Georgia peach."

"Charmed," I stated as I grabbed my clutch and walked away slowly.

"They say never trust a big booty and a smile," he commented. "What the hell does that mean?" he asked as he walked behind us.

"Just means nice to meet you," I answered in an irritated tone.

"I see that you're the mean one," he chuckled. "Don't matter, I like them mean and it's a challenge for me baby. Do you know who I am?"

"Am I supposed to drop my panties right here on the dance floor?" Kandice retorted.

"I'm just saying, I been checking you out since you got in here and you ain't gave anybody no play…so what's up with that?"

"Boy, bye," Kandice stated as she waved him off and walked away. I rolled my eyes at her as she kept walking.

"I really love your music," I stated as he stared at my ass.

"That's what's up," he replied. "Is that your friend or something?"

"My sister," I answered. "And she just doesn't do the whole ratchet scene."

"I can dig it," he stated. "So, do you know anyone in here?"

"No, I don't," I answered. "We are from out of town and I heard your music on the radio and I've been a fan ever since."

"Oh, really?"

"Yeah and when I heard that you were going to have a party here tonight...well I just had to come."

"That's cool."

"We need the man of the hour to come and get this bitch lit!" the DJ yelled on the mic.

"Well, I have to go but why don't you and your mean ass sister come to the after party?"

"I have one even better for you. Why don't you come to room 413 when you're done getting the crowd lit, and we can get lit together." I placed our room key in his hands as I kissed his cheek. "My pussy already wet," I whispered into his ear as I walked away.

I walked out of the conference room and headed towards the elevator until I was stopped by the concierge. "Ma'am, were you driving the Bentley?" he asked.

"Who's asking?" I asked rudely.

"It was in the fire lane and they are about to tow it," he retorted as he pointed to the front.

"Oh, shit!" I exclaimed as I practically ran through the sliding doors.

CHAPTER 11

Kandice

$\mathcal{I}$ really wasn't in the partying mood, so I decided to go up to our room for a little bit. *It didn't seem like it would be hard to get Dameon up to our room,* I thought to myself as I called up my boo. I couldn't wait to hear his voice and more importantly, I couldn't wait for my man to touch me. It had been months and my body missed him.

"Hey baby," he answered.

"Hey love, how is the packing going?" I inquired.

"Good, not bringing anything but my clothes and shoes. I am starting over fresh and I am so ready to protect the innocent and save lives."

"I know you're ready baby and I'm ready to see you. I can't wait to be in your arms," I mentioned.

We talked for about twenty minutes and I ended up dozing off. I guess I was still tired and had jetlag because I was sound asleep quickly until I felt a hand over my arm.

"You're back early?" I asked as I yawned with my eyes still closed.

"I ended up falling asleep and getting out of that tight ass dress."

"Great, then we can get straight to business," Dameon replied.

I jumped up quickly to see Dameon standing in front of me with his shirt off. He was staring at my body as I covered myself with the cover that was on the bed. "Damn, I must be getting the two for one special," he smiled as he walked closer to me.

"You need to leave right now!" I yelled.

"Oh naw baby, this party is just getting started. Where is your sister?"

"How the fuck did you get in here?" I asked, holding onto the cover with a tight grip over my body.

"Your sister gave me the key, so I assumed she gave it to me for a reason," he explained.

I stared into his eyes and saw nothing but pure evilness. My machete was in my bag near the sink and I had no way to get to it. It was the first time in my life that I felt helpless since my grandfather raped me. He moved closer to me and the room was so quiet that I could hear my heart beating through my chest. I swallowed my spit as he slowly moved closer.

"Get away from me," I yelled.

"This won't take but a second," he stated. "You were all talk downstairs and now you have nothing to say. I know about pretty ass yellow-bone bitches like you."

"Please don't do this," I pleaded.

"Bitches like you think you all-of-that and shit, right?"

"No, I don't."

"Yea you do," he laughed. "You thought you was going to come to my event and turn people down like you the shit."

"It's not like that," I stated. "Please just let me go and no one will ever have to know about this."

"Bitch, do you know who the fuck I am?" he chuckled. "Do you know how many bitches that I have and can get? Do you really think that people are going to believe that I raped you? Hell naw, I'm a fucking legend in these streets of Dallas and no one is going to believe your ass."

"If you rape me, they will have no choice after the rape kit," I explained.

"You're a groupie and we fucked so you got mad because I told you that I was married and you thought that you had won the lottery when you fucked with me."

"You're a lying bastard."

"My word against yours," he stated as he pushed me on the bed so hard that I hit my head on the headboard base.

He hit the light switch quickly as I tried to dart to the door, but I wasn't fast enough and he tackled me on the bed in the dark. "Shhhh," he stated with the pillow over my face. He ripped my panties off and flipped me over like I was nothing.

"Bet that pussy good," he laughed as he stuck two fingers inside of me. I could feel him un-zipping his pants as I squirmed all over the bed, fighting for my life until he hit me in the back of my head and everything went dark.

CHAPTER 12

Dameon Revenge So Sweet...

I was completely pissed off as I pressed the number four on the elevator button. I had to practically fight with the hotel staff and plead for them not to tow the Bentley that I rented. I just didn't need the hassle tomorrow when we were on our way back home. I just wanted to drop the rental back off and catch our flight back.

I searched my purse for the other key to the room and heard a strange noise as I put my ear to the door. It sounded like someone was fighting as the headboard shrieked against the wall. I opened the door quickly and hit the light switch, and was petrified as I saw Kandice's lifeless body and Dameon on top of her. I didn't know if he had raped her or not but I grabbed the first thing that I could spot, which was an iron, and hit him on the head with it. His body went limp as he fell to the floor. I noticed that he wasn't naked and his dick wasn't even hard, so he couldn't have raped her yet.

"Wake up," I shook Kandice as she was face down in the pillow.

She wouldn't budge for anything so I turned the water on in the sink and placed a cup under it. I threw the cup of cold water on her head and she woke up.

"Ahhhh!" she hollered.

"Are you okay?" I asked as I hugged her tightly. "Just seeing him on top of you and about to rape you makes me want to kill him in the worst way."

We both stared at him as she stood up from the bed. She went inside of the closet to get her bag and put on her pants.

"He should be waking up soon," I stated as I continued to look at him.

"He can't get away with this," Kandice retorted as she walked around to open her bag.

"Let's drag him into the bathroom," I stated.

"He's a heavy ass man," she blurted. "How the fuck are we going to do that?"

"Just improvise before he wakes up because he needs to be tied up and gagged."

"Okay," she stated as she followed my lead.

We worked together as a team to drag his lifeless body into the bathroom, removing all of his clothes, shoes, and socks as we used the rope in her bag to tie his hands onto the shower rod. The shower rod was actually good and sturdy because it held him.

"Go to the hardware store across the street and get duct tape," I demanded.

"Okay, anything else?"

"2 X 4 lumber, just one and a bat if they have one."

"I'll be back," she retorted. "Are you sure you want me to leave you alone with this animal?"

"I can handle it from here," I stated gracefully.

Kandice came back twenty minutes later and Dameon was still sleep with his hands in the air, hanging from the shower rod that was mounted into the ceiling. I grabbed the duct tape from Kandice and placed it in his mouth. I put my ear to his chest and the mutherfucker was still breathing, so we were still in business.

"They only had the bat," Kandice explained.

"Even better," I chuckled as I grabbed it from her.

I splashed his face with water a few times before he woke. He looked at me as his eyes were bloodshot red.

"It's safe to say that some shit will never ever change," I chuckled out loud as I held the bat. "You see, ten years ago, we went to school together. I'm not from New York stupid, I'm from Dallas just like you and I'm here for my revenge."

I ripped the tape off his mouth. "Ahhhhhhhh!" he hollered as I turn the water on scorching hot. He tried to wiggle out the rope but had no luck as we watched him.

"You stupid ass bitches! I don't fucking know y'all and you dumb bitch, I didn't go to school with you," he stated with authority as he eyeballed me.

"I beg to fucking differ, Dameon," I smiled. "You don't remember the dark skin girl that you and your fucking friends raped?"

"Charisma?" he asked in shock.

"You're got damn right," I acknowledged. "Live in the mutherfucking flesh and I grew up to be a savage because of heartless niggas like you." I paced the bathroom floor as I continued to talk. "You created this monster."

"So, what the fuck are you going to do to me bitch?" he asked in anguish.

"I want you to feel exactly what the fuck I felt," I stated with my hand on my head in a thinking manner. "If my memory serves me right, I believe it was you that decided to rape me in my ass. Your voice stayed in my head for years and the pain; it's something that I could never forget."

"We thought you killed yourself," he laughed as he looked up to see my facial expression.

"I'll be back," Kandice stated. "I'mma make sure that no one can hear us and check the halls to make sure no one is looking for his ass."

I slapped his face as he spat on my cheek. "You want to play, mutherfucker!" I yelled in anguish. "All of your so-called friends are dropping like fucking flies and do you know who did it? Me. Alex is dead. Carter is dead. You're about to be dead and that leaves only Charles and Amauri.""

"Get a grip on your life dumb ass girl. Instead of finding and killing us, why don't you get your life together. We didn't give a fuck about your ass so we did what we wanted. It was ten years ago and you need to live your fucking life," he spat.

"You must be stupid if you think I'm going to let you dumb shits walk around free after you did this to me."

Kandice walked back in and stared at me as she placed the hotel key card back into her bra. "It's all clear down there. Everybody lit and partying. It's so loud that no one can really hear him scream," she assured me.

"Great, hand me the tape."

I put a giant strip on his mouth again as he began to squirm. "Oh, don't squirm now mutherfucker," I laughed.

I opened my bag, grabbed the baby oil out of it, and poured it on the end of the bat. Dameon began to try to move, squirming rapidly as I walked closer to him. "Try to hold his legs," I mentioned to Kandice.

I rammed the end of the bat up his ass and moved it around like it was a dick. I wanted him to feel all of the pain that I had to endure. "You like that baby, is it good?" I teased. He was no longer squirming as blood and feces were scattered on the end of the bat and he peed all over the floor. I kept ramming it inside of him until Kandice threw the bat out of my hand.

"I think we've done enough here; it's time to go," she explained. With tears streaming from my eyes, I walked over and pulled the tape off his mouth. I took the small blade from my bra and cut his throat, watching as his blood made a puddle on the floor.

"It wasn't Amauri," he whispered as his head turned sideways. I knew he was dead as I stood there staring at him. I hadn't noticed that Kandice had packed all of our stuff.

"Let's go," she stated as she pushed me. "Snap out of it," she demanded as she practically pulled me to the elevator.

"I need the Bentley please," she told valet as he ran to get the car.

I didn't say anything the entire ride back to my house. We packed up whatever belongings we had and picked an earlier flight the next morning. All I could think of was what Dameon had said in his last breath, and I needed to know exactly what he meant. It was on my mind heavily.

CHAPTER 13

Charles Porter...

*H*ome sweet home, I thought as I grabbed the Sunday Times newspaper from the ground as I pulled the side of my robe to tighten it together. I plopped down on the couch and put my feet up while Kandice was in the kitchen cooking breakfast. The aroma from the bacon was making me super hungry as my stomach growled loudly.

I tried to keep my mind off it as I turned the newspaper around to the first page and there was an article about Charles. His picture was plastered on the front; apparently, he had been robbed and shot in the head. I held my mouth with shock as I continued to read.

Dallas native and quarterback for the New York Giants, Charles Porter, was murdered last night. He was last seen driving his Bentley after he left a party. A witness stated she saw him being held at gunpoint at a red light as the robbers shot him and took off in his car. She called the police in a hurry and stayed on the scene until the NYPD arrived. He was pronounced dead on sight with two bullets to the head. His family has stated that his body will be shipped to Dallas where they can have a proper burial for him. He leaves behind five-year-old twin boys and a fiancée, whom he planned to marry in his hometown next month.

"What a tragedy," I said out loud in a dramatic tone as Kandice brought me a plate with a cup of orange juice.

"What are you talking about?" Kandice asked.

"The fact that Mr. Charles Porter is dead," I smiled.

"Okay," she hunched her shoulders. "Who is that?"

"He was next on the list," I explained.

"Wow, are you fucking kidding me?"

"I guess that plan is out the door."

"Well, I was down for whatever; you know I'm not good on all the names and everything, but once we collab on a plan we're set," Kandice assured me.

"I know, and I have to admit that I am relieved that Charles was murdered," I smiled. "It takes time to do what we do and the fact that four of them are out of the way makes things so much better for me."

Kandice smiled as she began to gobble her breakfast. Poor girl was eating so fast like she was still inside of the mental institution. I decided that it was time to finally go into the office and get some major work done.

I drove my car to work and parked it with valet as I pressed the button for the elevator. My phone dropped out of my purse and I bent over to pick it up as the doors opened.

"Lachelle?" Karen practically screamed loudly. "I've been trying to get a hold of you to give you your check," she tried to explain.

I was in complete loss for words and tried to act like I didn't know her as the elevator doors shut.

"It's been a while," I replied.

"Yes, after someone murdered Mr. Strong I knew that it touched you. He talked so much about how you were the best assistant that he ever had and wanted to hire you on full time."

"It was just too much for me; surely you understand?"

"Of course I do, it's been a hard couple of months. My husband was murdered as well so I decided that it was best for the kids and I to just go back home."

"Home?" I inquired.

"Well, I'm from Dallas and New York is not the place for me."

"I completely understand and I hate to be rude, but I really have to go," I stated as I made my way to the elevator.

"Wait? What about your check?"

"You're right," I replied with a fake smile as I took a pen and envelope out of my purse. "Here's my address, so when you get a chance just send it there and I wish you well in Dallas."

"Thanks so much," Karen stated as she grabbed the envelope from my hands.

I scurried on the elevator and waited until I reached my floor. Conner, the security guard, was eyeing me as usual. I guess after killing mostly everyone who raped me, I could see clearly. Conner was extremely handsome and I can't believe that I never noticed him. He was dressed in a suit today instead of his normal security guard uniform. I never paid attention to his nice build, grey eyes, and full lips. This light skin brother had me at hello. I was feeling like I did when I was a freshman in high school and I didn't know why I was acting this way.

"You look different," I stated boldly as I walked closer to him.

"I'm sure everyone looks different outside of work," he replied.

"True, but I have to admit that you are killing that suit," I complimented.

"Thanks, I thought I'd come up here looking like money for my last day of work," he chuckled.

"Well you do look like money."

"I haven't seen you in a while," he noticed.

"Yea, there was a family emergency and I needed to take some time and get myself together."

"I hear yah," he replied. "I had to get myself together as well. I'm starting off as a rookie with the NYPD and I am getting an advancement."

"Protect and serve, right?" I smiled.

"Nothing but," he laughed.

"So, you wasn't going to tell me that you're leaving?"

"You been gone, so you know how that goes," he inquired as he grabbed his briefcase heading towards the elevator.

"How about a farewell dinner?" I blurted out.

He smiled as he turned around. "A farewell dinner for me?" he asked in surprise.

"I've been told that I am a great cook, so if you aren't busy why don't you come to my condo on Saturday night?"

"Wow, I would love to."

"Cool," I smiled, showing off my pearly whites. "Here is my address." I wrote it down on a piece of paper for him as I trotted into my office, leaving him staring at my ass in the tight black skirt.

I powered on my computer as I placed my briefcase on the desk and closed my door. It was about to be a long day of work and my search for Amauri wasn't going good, so I had no clue how long it would take me to find him. I began to think of things to cook as I waited for my computer to boot.

Later on that night...

"Hey girl," I shouted as I opened the door to the condo with my keys. "How did job hunting go?" I asked Kandice as she sat on the couch with her laptop in her lap.

"I've submitted a few applications but no one is biting," she stated with sadness. "I have no job experience, so it's really hard."

"I understand the job market is tough and not to mention the economy isn't looking good at this moment for jobs," I mentioned. "But, don't stress about that; guess what?"

"What?" she asked.

"I have a date Saturday night with an ex co-worker."

"Bitch, what?" she stated loudly.

"Shhhh, be quiet girl, I'm sure Brooklyn can hear you," I goofed.

"Shut up," she took a cheap jab at my arm. "Tell me how this unfolded because I can't believe you are going on a date."

"Well, we aren't going anywhere. I thought a nice, candlelight dinner here would suffice."

"Wow, it must be snowing outside," Kandice stated as she peeped out the blinds to check the weather.

"I know right, but it was like something just came over me today. I just went for it. I been ignoring this man for years and he's been practically begging for my attention. So, when he told me that it was his last day, I thought I'd ask him to come over for a farewell dinner."

"Sounds good to me, and you will get to meet my honey," Kandice winked.

"Oh, so Mr. Man is in town now?"

"He called me today and told me that he has an early flight on Saturday morning and he wants to see me that night."

"Damn, he ain't even going to unpack before he get to that pussy," I chuckled.

We both laughed and joked as I ran my bubble bath. I couldn't wait to soak as I jumped in and turned the water off. So many thoughts were in my mind as I sat in the jacuzzi tub. Life had changed so much for me after my mother died. My aunt was living somewhere in Jamaica with her husband and kids. I just didn't know what else there was for me to do in this life. I had no one but Kandice and nothing could eliminate our bond.

CHAPTER 14

Date Night...

Saturday night had finally arrived and I couldn't be more ecstatic. I had to admit that I had been masturbating for years and I guess I was finally tired of it. I just didn't know how it would feel to actually have a man kiss me. I had so much stress to be relieved and I felt that Conner was the perfect man.

Kandice was sad because her boo thang's mother passed, so he had to stay where he was until he buried his mother properly. He would be in New York in two weeks, right on Valentine's Day, so she was excited about that.

"Are you sure you don't want me to stay and hang around?" she asked as she walked towards the door in her red dress and pumps.

"Positive," I replied as I pulled the dinner plates out of the cabinet and set the table.

"Okay, well I'm off to this club to see how it is and shit," she stated as she opened the door. "Let me know if you need me; you know that I'm only one call or text away."

"I already know this," I declared as I smacked her ass while she went out the door.

I took a shower, rubbed my body down in *Bath & Body Works*, and slipped on a purple dress with the shoulder hanging off.

Knock. Knock. I looked at myself in the mirror one more time as I walked through the kitchen and caught a whiff of the fried chicken and tetrazzini.

"Damn," Conner stated as he stared at me.

"Something wrong?" I asked.

"Nothing could possibly be wrong with you; you're perfect."

I blushed hard as I closed the door behind him as he entered. He was looking nice in his white blazer and black slacks. I don't know what fragrance he was wearing but it smelled so good as I walked behind him.

We ate dinner, talked about life and began to drink wine. He kept looking at me as I tried not to blush.

"You know I've always had a crush on you," he mentioned as he took a sip of his wine.

"I knew," I replied as I stood up and crossed my leg over his leg.

"What are you doing?" he asked as I kissed his neck.

"I want you to fuck me."

"What?" he asked in shock. "I don't fuck, I make love."

"Well, I want you to make love to me."

"Are you sure that's what you want?"

"Positive," I replied as I pulled my dress off completely and it fell to the floor.

"Damn," he hissed. "How can I say no to that?"

I grabbed him by his hand and led him to my bedroom. Ten years was a long time and my body was in need of pleasure. I lay on the bed as he held my hand, while kissing the palm delicately.

"Why are you so romantic?" I sighed as I grabbed my hand back.

"Why are you so mean and hard to let someone in?" he asked as he grabbed my hand again.

I laughed slightly as he kissed my cheek. "Honey, if I told you my life story you wouldn't even understand it."

"I want to know about you," he pleaded.

"Not tonight," I stated. "I want you inside of me because I trust you will take care of me."

"I hope you're not looking for that rough loving because that's not my style."

"Give me your best," I added as he kissed my lips softly and we fell on the bed completely. He rubbed his fingers through my hair as I kissed him back. "You're so beautiful baby, like a work of art. I love this melanin skin that you're in." Slowly, he kissed my neck and worked his tongue all the way down to my navel. He circled his finger around my navel as he took my black velvet thong off with his teeth. I couldn't help but to be nervous as he spread my legs apart like Lamborghini doors.

"What are you doing?" I asked, bashfully.

"I'm eating dessert," he stated as he kissed both sides of my inner thighs and French kissed my pussy lips like it was really a dessert. He opened the lips and sucked on my pearl like it was a cherry as I grabbed the sheets on the bed and my toes curled. It was the first time I felt my body explode and I liked it. My body was shaking and trembling as he continued to suck and slurp all of my juices.

"God!!!" I screamed as I tried to close my legs.

"Oh no, baby, you gone take this." He smiled as he opened my legs and continued to suck on my cherry as I came repeatedly. I came so hard on his face that I thought I was having a seizure and going into convulsions.

After he was done, I lay on the bed trying to catch my breath as he kissed my forehead. "That was just a sample," he stated as he grabbed my hand and placed it on his dick.

"Damn," I hissed as I stood up.

"I want our first time to be special and I have a feeling it will be," he stated as he walked towards the door.

"Wait, where are you going?" I asked as I stood up from the bed.

"I'm going home to get some rest. It's getting late and I do have work in the a.m."

"Did I do something wrong?"

"Of course not. I'll definitely be back but I want us to get to know each other a little more. I want to know everything about you," he tried to convince me. "You will be mine and I am going to do whatever it takes to make you mine. You're not seeing anyone, right?"

"Of course not."

"Good."

I kissed his lips and walked him to the door as we said good night to each other. *Damn, was I dreaming or what?* I thought to myself as I locked the door.

CHAPTER 15

Happy Valentine's Day...

"Why are you moping around?" Kandice asked me as she brought me the mail from the mailbox.

"I'm not," I explained. "It's just been a week since I've seen Conner."

"Oh, let me find out that you being soft on this Conner dude," she teased.

"Girl, he sucked the soul out of me."

"I'm taking it that you never had your soul sucked out of you before."

"Your guess is right," I added in. "I haven't had a man since then and you know that."

"I be forgetting Charisma."

"All them damn drugs at the mental place," I chuckled.

"Bitch, fuck you!" she laughed.

"Seriously though, there is nothing to celebrate on Valentine's Day for me. The memories that I have from this day will forever be on my mind."

"I understand," she stated as she kissed my cheek. "Well, at least you will get to meet my boo because he's on his way over."

"Great," I replied sarcastically.

"Stop tripping girl."

"I will as soon as we get the last bastard on the agenda."

"I'm sure we will. Just don't think about this shit tonight. Why don't you go text your boo?"

"I am going to do that." I laughed as I looked at my phone. "I'm going to take a hot bubble bath and relax."

I sat in the bathtub almost an hour when I heard a knock at the door. I placed my ear buds on as I put my *Pandora* on the 90s R&B station. I found myself falling asleep and woke up thirty minutes later when the station's commercial had gotten louder. I grabbed my towel as I placed my phone on the sink and dried myself off.

I heard Kandice laughing away and knew she was drunk and enjoying herself. I didn't want to interrupt, so I thought that I would just go to my room without her seeing me until I heard a familiar voice.

I stopped in my tracks as I stared at Amauri sitting on the couch.

"Are you okay, girl?" Kandice asked as she looked at me. "You look like you've seen a ghost."

"It's nothing."

I closed my door as I searched my dressers for the blade. My heart was beating so fast as I paced back and forth. I couldn't believe this nigga was in my house and sitting on my couch. I didn't know what to think and it sucked that Kandice was with him now. He was as handsome as ever but I had to forget about that and remember the hatred that I had for him.

I peeked out of the door and Kandice was sitting on top of him, straddling him with her clothes on as she kissed his neck. "I don't know what's wrong my sis tonight," she stated as he had a big grip on her ass.

I grabbed my phone off the dresser and texted her.

Me: Bitch…come here now!

Kandice: I'm about to get some good dick. Not right now, bitch.

Me: It's an emergency.

I waited about ten minutes, pacing back and forth until Kandice walked in. "What's up with you tonight? Are you cockblocking or what?" she giggled.

"I wish I was," I replied.

"So, what's up?" she asked with her hands on her hips.

"Is his name Amauri?"

"Yea, why?"

"He's the fifth."

"The fifth?" she inquired, thinking about what I had just said. "Oh my god!"

"Ssshhhh!" I stated as I grabbed her quickly. "He didn't rape me but he set me up."

"Let's fuck him up," she stated as she turned the knob on the door to leave.

"Noo," I grabbed her by her hand. "Not like this; it has to be done right."

We came up with a plan together in ten minutes. She walked out of the room with nothing on as he turned around in amazement. The door was open slightly as I peeked out of it and waited for the cue.

"I missed you so much, baby." She kissed his neck as he rubbed her breast.

"I missed you too, baby," he said.

"I wanted to give you a special treat this Valentine's Day and make it one that you will never forget."

"Oh, really and how is that?" he smiled.

Kandice winked as he saw me walking out of the room. "Damn," he licked his lips in approval. I wore a lace negligee with the garter to match.

Kandice stood up and moved back as I kissed his neck and ears.

"Damn, I feel like I know you or something. Your eyes are telling me a story," he stated as he kissed my breast.

"Can I tie you up?" Kandice asked as she placed a rope around his feet as we walked him over to the chair. I placed the handcuffs over his wrists as I kissed his lips.

"This is some freaky shit," he smirked. "Two fine ass women handcuffing and tying me up is crazy, but I have no complaints at all. I have chocolate and a red-bone; the best of both worlds."

"You're funny," I told him as I bent down.

"Are you sure we haven't met?" he asked.

"Positive," I confirmed. "I'm just going to put this blindfold on you for a bit."

I put the blindfold over his eyes and gave Kandice a high-five as I slapped her ass. "Amauri, right?" I asked.

"Yes," he answered.

"I wanted to let you know that you fucked over the wrong bitch," I stated as I took the burning candle and poured the wax on his chest.

"Ahhhhh," he yelled. "What type of freaky shit is this? I'm not with this."

"I wasn't with it either ten years ago when you set me up."

"What the hell are you talking about? I don't know you."

"Oh, you know me very well."

I yanked the blindfold off his head as he stared at me with fear. "You had me all fucked up in the head and I believed that you actually cared about me."

"What the hell are you talking about?" he asked in a surprise tone.

"Dallas? Dorcy Academy?"

"Charisma!" he shouted.

"You're damn right," I replied.

"I looked for you for so long and I wondered what happened to you."

"Cut the shit," I replied as I slapped his face. "You know exactly what them bastards did to me."

"What are you talking about?" he asked.

"Why are you playing stupid like you don't know what the fuck happened? Valentine's Day you set me up."

"I don't understand."

"You set me up to get raped by your pathetic friends."

"What? I didn't set you up. I didn't know what happened to you. I was ran over that night in a hit and run. Hell, I can't even play football again because of the accident."

"Liar!" I screamed. "Do you know what the fuck I went through after that? I tried to kill myself because I was raped by four stupid, peon ass boys."

"I'm sorry, I didn't know," he pleaded. "I cared about you for real."

"He's got to be telling the truth, Charisma."

"Why do you say that?" I asked.

"Because the motherfucker has been telling me that story since I met him in the mental place," Kandice replied. "He told me a while ago that he was in a hit and run that kept him from going pro. It has to be some truth to it because every time we're together he mentions it."

"It's true, Charisma, I would never hurt you," he pleaded.

"Are you saying that all these years I thought you set me up and I hated you, it wasn't true?"

"I never had anything to do with it. They are probably who ran me over that night."

"I'm convinced they were the ones who did it, too," Kandice intercepted.

"If I could kill those bastards and get away with it," he shook his head in disbelief, "I would."

"Oh, they are all dead," Kandice chuckled.

"What?"

"It's true," I commented. "We devised a plan together and we've been killing those mutherfuckers one by one. I went to a plastic surgeon to get my face done so no one would ever notice me, and our plan succeeded."

"Let me go, please," he begged. "I promise you that I didn't have anything to do with what those pricks did to you. I wish I could have been there with you that night and protected you. I got a call from Dameon telling me that everyone was going to meet at our favorite store that we used to stop at after practice. I waited and no one came, but then I was hit by a car as I crossed the street. Everything makes sense now. Charisma, you have to believe me."

I looked in his eyes and knew he was telling nothing but the truth. It felt good to know all of these years that Amauri really had nothing to do with it all along.

"How do I know that you won't turn us in?" I asked.

"My word is bond. I took an oath to protect and serve and I won't remember anything that was said tonight."

I don't know what took over me but I kissed Amauri. Kandice pushed me off him and looked at me. "He's mine," she stated with authority. "Now that we know he had nothing to do with it."

"He was mine first," I teased as I kissed him again. "Come and join me."

Kandice walked over, grabbed my head, and kissed me wildly. Amauri's eyes were so big as he watched us kiss and feel on each other. I reached down to his pants to unzip them, and the monster he had between his legs was already as hard as Chinese arithmetic. I stroked his hardness as I looked into his eyes and bit my bottom lip.

I pulled his pants down as he sat on the chair, still handcuffed. "I want him," I told Kandice as she helped me to pull off my thong and garter.

"Just get on top of him and ride him slowly until the pain goes away," Kandice demanded.

I did as instructed as I held on to his chest and sat on his lap as I teased the tip of his dick with my wetness. The head went in and I wanted to stop as the pain began, until Kandice came over and began to kiss me on my neck. "You got this, just keep riding our dick," she whispered in my ear. He was at least ten inches with thickness and half of him could barely get inside of me.

"Shitttt," he moaned as I bounced up and down slowly. "It's so good," he kept repeating as he kissed my breast. "Un-tie me."

We un-tied his feet and let him out of the handcuffs as he made both of us lay on the bed. He began to suck on my pussy as he played with Kandice's clit. We were both moaning as we held hands and came together. "Let me fuck this pussy like I always wanted to," he demanded as he picked me up and entered me.

"Oh my," I screamed as he worked himself inside of me slowly.

"Fuck!" he moaned as he pounded away at my pussy.

Kandice was watching at this point and playing with her clit as she bit her bottom lip.

"Damn this pussy so good," he stated as he put me back on the bed, pulling my legs all the way to my head. Kandice stood up and began to stimulate my clit with the lipstick vibrator while he was inside of me stroking away. I held onto the sheets as he continued to fuck me.

"Yes!" I screamed as my body went into convulsions and I squirted all over the both of them.

"Damn," Kandice smiled. "My turn," she stated as she patted him on the back.

The next day...

I woke up with nothing but sweet dreams knowing that I was finally in a good place. Amauri didn't have anything to do with my rape and Kandice and I had a very good night. It was better than I could have ever expected. I felt something gushy on my hands and woke up to see Amauri lying next to me with his throat slashed and blood covered completely on my hands.

I jumped up crying and screaming with my entire body filled with his blood. Kandice was laying right next to him and I cried as I walked over to her to see her throat slashed as well. I checked her pulse as I went ballistic and screamed uncontrollably. She was dead. Tears streamed down my face as I grabbed a bat from under my bed.

I looked up to see Conner staring at me at the door, as he rubbed the knife with his finger. His eyes told a story of evilness as he stood there in silence.

"I thought you said that you were single?" Conner asked, staring at me as he wiped off his knife. I swallowed my spit as I stared at Conner.

"I am single," I stated as I nodded in shock.

Conner walked up closer to me with the knife still in tow as he pulled me by my hair. He took a long whiff of my hair.

"Why are you doing this?" I asked as he held my head.

"Because I waited years for this moment. You have no idea what I went through to find you. I went through hell and back trying to get your attention and you never noticed me. Ten years ago all I wanted was your attention and I knew you would be mine from the moment I met you."

"What? I don't know you."

"You're right, you don't know Conner, but you do remember Dion, right?"

"Dion?" I tried to remember but couldn't.

"Yes, I thought we shared something special back home in the ward in Dallas."

"Oh my god!" I screamed.

"Yes, I changed everything about myself to find you and be with you, and now that I have you….I will never let you go..." he stated as he threw me on the floor.

I fell hard to the floor on my stomach as I saw my pistol under the bed. I grabbed it quickly and shot him one time in the head. Blood poured from his wound as he fell down to the floor and landed directly on top of me. I lay there breathing heavily as tears dropped from my eyes. I waited for almost twenty seconds to make sure he was dead. Slowly, I pushed his body from on top of mine and ran into the bathroom to grab a damp towel to clean my body and face. I stared at myself in the mirror as I continued to cry. I knew it was time for a change and for the first time in my life, I didn't know what to do.

I put on my jogger set and placed as many clothes as I could in my luggage. Before I left out the door, I walked over to Kandice's body and kissed her cold cheek delicately. She looked like sleeping beauty and I cried as I said my last good-bye.

"We been through so much together," I cried as I placed the comforter over her naked body and walked away.

Five hours later...

"Hello beautiful, welcome to Jamaica," the desk agent said as I walked off the plane into the terminal desk station. "May I have your I.D. for luggage check in?"

"Sure." I opened my wallet and hesitated as I flipped through both I.D.'s. It felt damn good to give her the identification that I was now proud of.

"Charisma?" she inquired. "What a beautiful name."

"Thank you."

"Is this your first time here or do you have family here?"

"I have family here," I stated proudly as I grabbed the post card out of my purse with my aunt's address and walked to the taxi outdoors.

THE END

AUTHOR NOTE

Kendra Rainey is a native of (Pleasant Grove) Dallas, Texas. She is a gutsy, courageous, and gifted voice that will soon take the urban literary community by storm. Kendra currently resides in Dallas and is the mother of two handsome boys. She works as a teacher, play-writer, and community advocate. She has written *A Bad Chick* (newly released as *Chronicles of a Bad Bitch), She in Love with His Coco-Tales of Dallas BBW, She in Love with His Coco 2, She Fell for the Realest 1* and *2*, and more. She is currently the CEO of Curvy Girl Publications, paving the way for curvy, plus-size, BBW women. To check out any of her other work, please visit her Amazon and other social media pages.

If you want to check out any of my other work, please check me out on my Amazon page.

SOCIAL MEDIA AND CONTACT INFO:

Twitter: www.witter.com/AuthorKendraR

Facebook: www.facebook.com/khalani.rainey

Kendra Rainey (Publisher)

Like page: www.facebook.com/AuthorKendraRainey/?fref=ts

Instagram: www.instagram.com/author_kendrarainey/

Email: authorkendrarainey@gmail.com or curvygirlpublications@gmail.com

Amazon: www.amazon.com/KendraRainey/e/B00ZAUUEAG/ref=sr_ ntt_srch_lnk_9?qid=1518210824&sr=1-9

CPSIA information can be obtained
at www.ICGtesting.com
Printed in the USA
LVOW10s2043200318

570524LV00017B/317/P